Ashes to Ashes, Oranges to Oranges

by

Eric Henderson

Illustrated by Marybeth Chew

Flickerlamp Publishing
Meriden, Connecticut

ASHES TO ASHES, ORANGES TO ORANGES

Words © 2014 Eric Henderson
Images © 2014 Marybeth Chew

The stories "Pizza Castle," "The Swimming Pool," "Peanut Butter Elvis," and "Nothing Concrete," originally appeared (in alternate form, under alternate titles) in the web-newsletter *The Frantic Flicker* and are © 2004, 2014 Eric Henderson.

A Flickerlamp Book
Published by:

Flickerlamp Publishing
P.O. Box 786
Meriden, CT 06450

www.flickerlamp.net

ISBN 978-1-940735-03-0

First printing: April, 2014

Printed in the U.S.A.

For my parents, who always encouraged me to
pursue my own interests.

Contents

"When you run out of iron, all you've got is rust.
When you run out of ashes, all you've got is dust.
Something something something oranges.
Something apples, also end in oranges."

-The Goat Butt Hair Cookbook

Make a New World Real

I grew up watching Carmine's choreography, just like everyone in my world did. But for me, he was different, special. It felt like destiny - from the age of ten or eleven, I knew he was the guy, that we would work together, and be together, too. Not that Carmine doesn't go out with other women occasionally, and of course I do what I want, but mostly we're together. We understand each other in a way that only great artists and their greatest muses can.

Still, when I moved to the city, I was surprised by how easy it was to get in touch with him. Of course, he had fallen out of favor quite a bit since the Daniel Hayes interview that made him seem like a monster.

Now, I'd like to talk about this "occult" business, since the basis for those accusations are what my story ends up being about. For the record, Carmine is not at all obsessed with the occult; he's obsessed with *science*. Specifically, he spent thirteen years or so (pretty much since I started dancing) working on a way to change the world through dance. When I say change the world, I don't mean he just wanted to motivate people to fix the environment or stop wars or anything like that. I mean he wanted to *physically* change the world as we know it by stretching the known laws of time and space. So that's what he was working on.

Carmine's theory was that human beings had a different kind of knowledge before written language was invented. He says dance was probably key to the development of written language, but once writing caught on, humans gained a higher level of individuality that kept them from focusing together (a group as a single unit) as well as before. It's a little more complicated than that, and I'm afraid I'm not always good at putting things in language that single-world people like yourself can understand. My job is to relay the facts - and here they are: written language killed transcendent dance, and that's why Carmine didn't read anything, has *refused* to read *any*thing, since before the millennium. I haven't read anything either (personally I just never got into it) and that was a bond between the two of us early on.

I know for a fact you've never heard of Daniel Hayes. If I wasn't involved like I was, I wouldn't remember him either. Hayes was a reporter, the one reporter to whom, for whatever reason, Carmine granted personal access at the absolute height of his success. Carmine was a very private person, and lots of people wanted to hear his story, but he gave it to *this* guy. Unfortunately for the world at the time, Hayes took that interview and turned it into an article that ended Carmine's mainstream career.

According to Carmine's agent at the time (who actually read the article), Hayes took Carmine's simple comments about science and history and distorted them just to cause a sensation. On finding out that Carmine held genuinely different beliefs from most of the public, Hayes led the conversation on and on

10

in that direction, until the final printed article insisted that Carmine was obsessed with the occult, devil worship, ritual sacrifice and even cannibalism. Yes, it's true that Carmine is interested in all of those things, a little bit, but as his best friend, confidante and lover for the past two years, you can believe me when I tell you he's not *obsessed* with any of them. That reporter had no business going near that stuff. Also, Carmine was pretty drunk when he did the interview, and that probably didn't help much either.

Flash forward seven years, and suddenly Carmine, now with me at his side, is on the verge of, not just the greatest triumph of his career, not just the greatest achievement of his life, but maybe the greatest scientific breakthrough in history.

It's a show, sort of. Carmine wrote, produced and directed it, as much as it needed those things, and of course he created the dance. The name of the show? "Make a New World Real," and here's how it works - it's one eighteen-minute routine, performed by fifteen women "up to" three times, "until it works."

Carmine put his own money into the project, and all of my money, too, all of *all* the girls' money. Maybe you're wondering how fifteen women could be convinced to put their life savings on the line and then work as hard as we did to master "Make a New World Real," without ever thinking "this guy must be an idiot- dancing can't break the fabric of time and space." It's a fair question, and the answer is that we're not scientists, we're dancers. And how many opportunities do you get, as a dancer, to participate in something that might be important to the whole world?

Carmine is the only person with these ideas. He's the only person who would ever do this. We didn't know if it would work, but we knew we believed in *him*. And what if it did work? What if it really was a historically significant experiment, like that guy who flew his kite in the rain and the key lit up and he discovered electricity?

As I mentioned, there were fifteen of us in the show. None of us knew each other except through Carmine. We all practiced individually, under his personal guidance. We danced to the music until we could dance without it. Then we teamed up into groups of three, and the magic started to happen. It wasn't really magic, though, was it? Just new science, Carmine said. It was me, Mary and Sukanya in the first group. We started on the routine and of course, Carmine's routines are difficult to begin with, but this one was cranked up to to near infinity, with these wild, forceful steps that made you wonder if anyone in the world had ever moved that way. So we were doing together exactly what we'd been practicing singly for a few weeks.

While the music played, everything seemed normal. Then, at a key moment, Carmine turned the music off... and immediately, the world started to wobble. Things got fuzzy and the three of us found the same place in our collective consciousness where it became difficult to focus on the dance, but it would have been even harder to stop it. Before the end, Mary dropped to one side. She saw something, she said, and maybe it was the end of the world.

To everyone's surprise, Carmine wasn't upset about her stopping - he smiled and laughed. He still hadn't told us what we were doing exactly, so none of us understood what the big highlight of the show was, what was going to "work" when we repeated these motions in a group of fifteen, in front of a crowd. I wondered if it really would be the end of the world.

So I asked him right then, right in front of everyone, "What are we doing, Carmine? What's the big idea behind all of this?" I'd never spoken to him like that before, but again, he was just beaming.

"Didn't I tell you? We're bringing back a dinosaur."

Without looking around at the other girls, I knew none of us were going to call him crazy. Of course, this information didn't gel with the world we knew, it didn't make any sense. But Carmine is the most amazing person I've ever met. If anyone could really bring back a dinosaur, it would be him.

"Do you think the dinosaur will have feathers, Cara? What color do you think its skin will be?"

"I don't know," I said.

"Neither do I," said Carmine, "At least not yet. Now let's get back to work"

By the night of the show, we were actually ready to make a dinosaur appear. We'd trained fully, both individually and in different configurations of three. And for the final phase, Carmine had us thinking about the dinosaur as well. There was a drawing of it, and Carmine gave each of us a copy to keep under her pillow. The dinosaur in the drawing was eight feet tall with red skin, razor sharp teeth and tiny arms. It did have feathers, on its tail, and on top of its head. We knew very well at which point in the proceedings we needed to be thinking about it. We were all on the same page.

The theater only held about three hundred people, but it was packed. Carmine let it be known that there would only be a single performance of "Make a New World Real," ever, and we heard rumors about physical altercations amongst the die-hards before the doors opened.

Our costumes were the perfect shade of dinosaur-skin red. As we were putting them on backstage, Carmine came in, looking amused. He announced that Daniel Hayes was in the audience. None of us knew what to say. We all understood that Daniel Hayes was the guy whose article led to the start of Carmine's troubles, but we didn't really know what that meant to Carmine.

There was no curtain in the theater, and the way the show begins is with all fifteen of us spaced evenly across the stage. Someone in the booth made a mistake, and the lights came on while we were still lining up. There was some light applause, and someone in the crowd started to giggle. The lights went out again, and then turned back on when they were supposed to. The applause began. We stood in our opening spots, looking amazing in crimson, and we could see that the crowd wanted to keep clapping, but had to stop themselves to relieve the anticipation. But then, from somewhere, there was that giggle again. It started the same as before, then grew quickly into one of the most maniacal sounds I've ever heard. It was horrendous, and all I could think about was how Carmine had said Daniel Hayes was there.

Then the music started, and my body's internal program took over. We'd never done the routine all together before, but it was an absolutely perfect performance. I was in the front, to the left, and every time the steps turned me so the other dancers were in view: only beauty, only perfection. We were still in the first few minutes, but already that air felt thick. It was clear to me that something extraordinary was happening.

Twelve minutes and nine seconds in, the music stopped in mid-measure, but as we'd practiced countless times, the dancing continued. It was a difficult moment in the routine, and it would become more difficult with each passing second until the piece was over, but we were ready. The world started to wobble, as it had before, and this time everyone could feel it. The crowd gasped. We were all leaving trails of light in the air - you could see our energy. We were frozen in motion, butter melting in a pan at 180 beats per minute.

And then, as we'd rehearsed, it was time to think about the dinosaur. It's eight feet tall, its skin is red, a crown of feathers on its head. And repeat!

It's eight feet tall, its skin is red, a crown of feathers on its head. Again!

Mere steps away, moving faster together than any of us could have moved alone - we were chemicals combining furiously, creating a reaction. I noticed Carmine, just offstage, performing in perfect harmony with all of us. "He's fifty-two years old," I thought, "What the hell is he doing?"

And at that very moment, when things couldn't possibly go on, and couldn't possibly stop, from somewhere in the crowd, once again, came that horrible, horrible giggle. And then the world broke.

When I regained consciousness, the roar of the crowd was deafening. Was it any later? No. I was still on stage, and still dancing, but going into the "cool-down" portion at the end of the piece. I was in the same costume, and dancing with the same girls as before, and there was still no music playing, but everything else was different. The new world was real.

The theater, and its crowd of three hundred, were gone. We were dancing outside, under the stars. When the number was over, I looked out into the darkness, and the crowd stretched as far as my eyes could see - there were thousands and thousands of people, all adoring, worshipful, all there for us, and for Carmine. We looked around at each other. We didn't see a dinosaur, but everything else was so different we didn't think to look for one. We wept, hugged each other close, and took our bows. It had only taken one try, and it had worked.

Then we saw Carmine. He was drinking champagne straight from the bottle and talking to a man that none of us recognized. He was laughing, and patting the man on the back. He noticed us, and came over to talk.

"That was my agent," Carmine said. "I didn't think I'd talked to him in several years, but evidently we've been together all along."

We were all thinking the same thing, but Katrina said it first, "Daniel Hayes?"

"Who?" said Carmine, smiling, "I don't think anyone around here has ever heard that name, certainly not in relation to me."

"We heard him laughing," said Britt.

"No, dear," said Carmine, "I'm sorry I had to pull that trick on you all. But once I stumbled on the idea, it seemed the easiest way. No, the giggler wasn't Hayes. Hayes wasn't really there at all, he didn't need to be. All I needed was for you to be focused on wanting him gone."

This explanation worked its way through the group of us slowly. Carmine took a swig from the champagne bottle, then turned and walked away. Everyone would understand eventually, or not, but that didn't mean he had to stick around until they did.

The press was assembled in front of the table on the dais, anticipating great words from the great man. As he entered the room, they all shouted questions at once. I caught up to Carmine and tugged on his sleeve. He turned to me and smiled.

"The dinosaur," I said.

Carmine stepped backwards away from me, and toward his place of honor.

"I'm the dinosaur, darling. I'm an eight-foot-tall red dinosaur, with sharp teeth and feathers on my head. And I'm back!"

The Truck

The bills were keeping Tom up at night. They'd put all of their savings into the move, and now everything else was falling apart. They'd been in Connecticut for 75 days, and now they were down to the last few hundred dollars on the last credit card. They were waiting for something to happen.

The first time he noticed the truck was on a Friday night. Their house was alone at the end of the road. There was no reason for anyone to drive down that far, unless it was someone they knew, and they hardly knew anyone in Connecticut at all. Tom's first thought was that it must be teenagers, drinking or drugging, having sex maybe. Tom refused to sympathize - he was only thirty, but a quick decade of money worry had wrung the whimsy out of him.

Whoever was inside, there it was, a big SUV-looking thing. Tom wasn't a car guy - cars were expensive, and they all got you the same place anyway, right? The truck was a dark color, black or blue, green maybe? You couldn't really tell at night. In fact, if not for the snow, he might not have noticed it at all.

The winter heating bills in Connecticut were yet another expense Tom hadn't foreseen. There had been oil in the tank when they'd moved in, but that would run out soon, and they weren't likely to be able to afford more before spring.

Worrying, pacing the floor, and eating constantly were Tom's hobbies, the things he had become best at, and lately he'd taken to looking out the window as well. Earlier that same night he'd caught himself at this latest trick, and called himself a fool.

"Ten thirty," he'd reminded himself, "when the collection guys show up in person, it'll be during business hours." Still, an hour later, he found himself looking outside again. And an hour after that, he noticed the truck.

The truck sat across the street, directly opposite the house, just idling. The windows were dark. As he stared out between the curtains, Tom thought that when they got some real money, when his play was a smash hit, the first thing they'd do would be

17

to get that same kind of UV filtering tint on all the windows of the house. That would keep all these nosy whoever-the-hell-they-were people from spying on them in the middle of the night. In the meantime, he decided to shut off the kitchen light until they went away.

"So, really, who could this be?" Tom thought. Right after they'd moved in, he and Linda had met the old man who owned the field across the street. He drove a ratty old pickup. Tom had discounted the idea of a bill collector earlier, but the thought snuck back now like a starving dog that's already been pushed away. They did owe a lot. Maybe all of their creditors had gotten together and hired a private detective to keep an eye on them. Surely they must have some money. No one could be as broke as they kept saying they were.

"Joke's on you, buddy," Tom said aloud, "We got nothin'." And whether this thought comforted him or numbed him, the next thing Tom knew, Linda was shaking his shoulder and telling him she was ready for her breakfast.

The telephone was another burden. They'd let their cell phones lapse during the move, and assumed it would only be a day or so before some money started coming in, and they could get them turned on again. Neither of them had been online for almost 3 months. The land line was on now due only to a single stroke of good luck: the house's former owner (a little old lady who'd moved into pre-hospice) had somehow forgotten to have it shut off. Of course they needed a phone in case someone called with a job for one of them, but that seemed less and less likely. They could recognize most of the collection agency numbers on the caller ID, and Tom even kept a list by the phone with the heading "Do not answer from!" But lately the telephone people had been calling, the bill wasn't being paid, and soon that would be gone, too. Soon that list he'd spent so long on would be more hard work down the drain. And anyone wishing to hire either of them would have to… what? Come by in person? They were screwed.

It wasn't that they didn't want to work – far from it. Linda had three good years of teaching experience before they moved, and Tom was still weighing his options, but he had nothing against the idea of employment. He'd gone of his own volition to sign up with the Ogilvie Temporary Service the week they'd arrived. Linda had made a fuss about him signing up to get a temporary job, instead of a regular one, and he'd had to explain it to her again. Explain that he was an artist, and that artists owe their time to their art, not some job.

Tom's art had not made the transition to Connecticut easily. In California, when he'd first moved there, he'd been able to write 15 or 20 pages of screenplay a day, and been incredibly productive. The hurdle had come when he realized that he wasn't any more interested in selling his products to Hollywood than Hollywood was interested in buying them. So, after hours of talks with Linda, and two sessions with an expensive career counselor, it was decided that once they made the move to Connecticut, Tom would become a playwright. Playwrights can write plays about anything, even things they care about, and no one will automatically think their plays are stupid and won't sell. They weren't online, but they did still have a computer, and Tom's first play was gradually starting to take shape.

Shortly after eleven on Monday night, Tom noticed the truck again. He didn't see it drive up, and if he hadn't checked many times over the weekend, he might have thought it had been there all along. The engine chugged steadily and the exhaust drifted out into the night, but it struck Tom as odd that he hadn't yet seen the truck actually move.

So really, now, who could it be? They had skipped the weekend, but now they were here again. He remembered telling the man at the gas station that his play was very political, but he was sure he hadn't mentioned which way it leaned politically. Could that geezer have assumed Tom's political affiliation, then gotten a nephew, or worse, hired someone to sit in front of his house to intimidate him into not creating a piece of art that no one would ever read or see anyway? Were the people in this town really that hard up for entertainment?

Then a new wave of thought crested in Tom's mind. Linda had been into town to the grocery probably a dozen times or more. Maybe this was her new stalker, even her boyfriend, come to pay unbidden respects to the lovely young lady sleeping upstairs. She was sleeping upstairs, wasn't she? At that thought, Tom leaped up. He took the stairs two at a time. He reached the bedroom door and listened. Nothing. He opened the door, and there was Linda, just as he'd left her when he'd tucked her in an hour and a half ago. He turned the light on, but she didn't stir. He looked under the bed, and checked the closet. No one there. The window was locked. Tom smiled. He kissed Linda on the forehead and then continued room to room, conducting a similar search of the rest of the premises. When he got back to the kitchen, the light was still out, and the truck was still parked across the street, idling.

Tom had a seat at the kitchen table. Whoever was out there, they were still out there, and that probably meant there was an ordinary, logical explanation. The light purr of the engine lulled him to sleep without further fanfare.

The next day, Tom thought long and hard about whether he should mention the truck to Linda. She had asked him something about sleeping in the kitchen two nights in a week, and he'd avoided the topic by mumbling something about that's where he felt most useful. Still, he knew she'd probably bring it up later, and he would have to give a better answer. Coming out and saying he thought their creditors were catching up to them would start an argument as quickly as saying they didn't need to put premium-grade gas in the car.

Linda would freak out: blaming, accusing, yelling, crying, blithering, and maybe even taking a detour towards the violent before she finally reached for the vodka and headed for bed. Then there might be weeks without the goodnight kisses or cheerful 'good morning's that were the highlights of Tom's Connecticut existence. So the subject had to be approached in just the right way.

"There was a truck out there," Tom said finally, having strategized through most of breakfast.

"What?"

"A truck, parked across the street with the engine running, just sitting there."

"What kind of truck?"

"I dunno. Just like a big SUV kind of truck. It was out there all night."

Linda frowned. "That's why you slept in the kitchen?"

"I fell asleep before they left, Friday night and last night, too. Pretty weird, huh?"

"Tom, I want you to re-read that time management book. I think we could be doing a lot better." This was the edge of the argument, and he'd have to parry and thrust just so to avoid it.

"Way ahead of you, babe," Tom said, "I've been highlighting it. A lot of good things in there. Helpful hints. Really helpful. In fact, I was planning on looking it over again today."

"But don't you think…"

"That my time would be better spent doing something else besides reading a time-management book?"

"Yeah."

"Well, you gotta know how to do it before you can, I think. Once I've read it a couple more times, I'll have better time-management skills than I'll know what to do with. Then we'll really be in better shape." Tom knew this was a deep stretch, but maybe…

"Okay. I just don't want this truck thing to take up too much of your time. You know we've got enough problems…"

"I know, honey. And working together, we're really going to solve them this time."

"I love you." Linda smiled, and Tom smiled back, as pleased with himself for having avoided a fight as with anything else. Although Linda hadn't added much insight to the truck situation, at least she knew about it now. And with the passages he'd already highlighted in the aforementioned time management book, Tom knew that soon Linda would go upstairs to read, and maybe take a nap or two, and that he would have the rest of the day to do as he pleased.

Later that afternoon, Tom and Linda made love for the first time since the move. The slack he'd been given in the morning had given him the extra oomph he felt he needed to seduce her.

Of course, it wasn't really much of a seduction. She had been reading when he came in. "What are you doing right now?" he'd said, and raised his eyebrows. Seduction complete.

After, they cuddled and napped, and Tom felt happier than he had in weeks. In their slumber, Tom and Linda both had the same dream, phrased differently, but with the same sense of longing. A big house, maybe even this house, with a yard and a perfect garden. Children, of course, well-adjusted: not without their problems, but good kids. A group of friends (remember friends?) who weren't boring or awful, with interests similar to their own. Esteem, respect, standing; a big wall of these things built up so high that the worst kind of scandal could never knock it down completely. Money.

When Tom woke up, it was dark outside. He let Linda sleep, and went downstairs for a snack. Snatches of the dream still fluttered through his mind, and he smiled as he entered the kitchen. He had found the love of his life, and together, some way or another, they would get there. It would all come true.

The truck sat just where it had before. But this time, when Tom saw it through the kitchen window, his resolve surprised him. Before he realized what was happening, the snack was forgotten; Tom had pulled a coat on over his bathrobe and slippers and was out the door. Crossing the street, almost to the truck, Tom rolled with it, consciously deciding not to think about how intimidated he'd felt before. He crossed the headlights, but couldn't make out anything through the windshield. He flashed a fat, phony smile at the person he imagined sitting in the driver's seat. Cheesing it up was never a bad idea – let 'em know you know they're there, and that you're ready to have a friendly chat.

As he reached the far side, the driver's side window, Tom realized how loud the truck really was. No wonder it had bothered him. He flashed that goofy smile again, and waited for the window to roll down. Nothing. Tom drew in a breath and rapped a knuckle on the window. Come on, he thought, whoever you are, let's get this over with. But there was no answer.

Tom looked out at the field across the street from his house. In the winter evening light he could see the pristine crust of two-day old snowfall – no tracks in the field or the ditch that he could see. It was cold, freezing. Tom knocked harder on the window. Still no answer.

In an effort to keep warm, Tom circled the truck quickly, watching the ground for tracks all the way around. He couldn't be sure in the dark, but he didn't think he saw any. He stopped at the driver's side door again and exhaled hard. He'd come this far, might as well settle it now. He reached out his hand for the door handle, and lifted it.

As Tom opened the door, the soft glow of the interior lights on the light brown upholstery and a sudden rush of heat reminded him of nothing so much as a Christmas hearth. It felt so overwhelmingly good that for a few seconds he forgot that he was looking into a stranger's vehicle parked in the street.

"Hello?" Tom said. No answer. He stepped up onto the outside step, so he could get a good look into the truck. No one in the front seat, no one in the back seat. He couldn't really see into the cargo hold in the back, but what would someone be doing back there?

"Hello?" he repeated. Tom relaxed a second. He held his hands in front of him, directly in front of the steering wheel, and rubbed them together. It wasn't a bad truck – it certainly seemed comfortable enough. Sure, he knew, any port in a storm, but still…

Tom turned suddenly, expecting someone to be behind him, but no one was. He jumped down, closed the door of the truck and headed back toward the house.

From the front of the truck, their little three-bedroom house looked positively massive. How had Tom been so lucky? He hadn't worked a full day at a real job in over five years, and now, thanks to Linda's devotion and just blind, dumb luck, this palace was his home. He hadn't really given any of it enough thought. He was living the American dream, and all he did was worry. He was rich. This truck, this possible intruder into their vast personal space was just another example of how Tom's worries were those of a wealthy man.

Tom smiled again as he climbed the stairs to the front door. He knew he could do better. Maybe he'd even call a real job agency tomorrow. That sounded like a good idea. A little hard work never killed anyone. He reached out his hand to open the door, but the knob wouldn't turn. It was locked.

Tom stood there in the freezing cold cursing for a moment or two. Waking up Linda was the last thing he wanted to do, but he guessed he would have to. He hoped that their little love-fest that afternoon would have her in a forgiving mood. He would even tell her about the job he was planning to get. Sure. Then he wouldn't be able to back out.

He drew in a breath and was about to start in with the loud banging, when the door opened in front of him. A man in pajamas stuck his head out.

"Can I help you?" the man said. The man was about Tom's size, and his posture was defensive.

"Who the hell are you?" Tom said. At that, the man's look turned from one of mild fear to a sort of astonishment. He laughed.

"Uh, who are you? We've been watching you three nights now, trying to figure out what you're up to."

Tom started to enter, but the man blocked his way.

"Hang on, man. We don't know you. You weren't invited in." Tom ignored this and continued pushing forward. The man pushed back, until Tom was once again on the doorstep.

"Linda!" Tom said, "Linda, are you okay?" Linda rounded the corner from the kitchen.

"Tom, what's going on?" she said.

"I'm not sure," said the man, "Do you know this guy?"

Tom and Linda looked at each other, but nothing passed between them. Tom tried again to make it through the door, but the man stood his ground. Linda screamed:

"Tom, do something!"

"Call the cops, Linda, this guy's on drugs or something."

"Why did you call him Tom? I'm Tom, Linda! I'M TOM!"

"Call 911!" the man pushed at Tom again, knocking him off of the steps, and onto his back in the snow. The snow bit from the bottom of Tom's robe to the backs of his heels, and the man was on top of him, putting him in a headlock.

Linda stood at the door, a cell phone in her hand.

"Tom, be careful," she said.

"Hold on, honey, it's okay," the man said, and then to Tom "Look, buddy, I'm gonna give you one chance, and you really ought to take it. I'm gonna let you go, and you get back in your truck, and you drive away, and if I ever see you again, if my wife ever sees you again, if we ever see your truck again, you're gonna be in a world of hurt. You got it?"

Tom had known Linda for twelve years. He had seen every expression her face was capable of making, and he knew what each of them meant. He knew that the look she had given him was real. This situation, whatever it meant, it was really happening. The man tightened his grip around Tom's neck.

"You got it? Otherwise, we're gonna call the cops and let them sort it out."

"I'm..." Tom started, but didn't know what else to say. In the scuffle, he had lost one of his slippers, and his foot was going numb. The pressure around his neck increased again.

"Last chance. Okay?" said the man.

"Okay," said Tom, "I'll go."

The man released his grip and backed up the stairs, but Tom didn't try anything else. Tom picked up his other slipper and put it on. He half-ran, half-scuttled across the street. As he reached the front of the truck, he turned.

"Goodbye, Linda," he said, loud enough for her to hear. Linda and the man stood in the doorway of the house. Her smile to Tom was flat, the kind you'd give someone at the end of a mismatched date:. "Goodbye, Linda," he said it again, under his breath.

The cab of the truck was as warm as he'd remembered. It smelled good, too, like soup and hot chocolate. He turned the key and heard an awful grinding sound – the truck was already turned on. There was a full tank of gas, and everything seemed to be in order.

There was no way to know what had happened, and no way to know what would. There was only Tom (or maybe not even Tom anymore) in the driver's seat. He knew instinctively that it was fair. That he'd squandered all he'd been given. He hadn't made any of the payments on time. It didn't matter what power had done it. His life had been repossessed, and all he knew was that it was right. Even though he knew they couldn't see him, he waved to Linda and Tom one last time. Then he put the truck into gear and headed out to the highway.

Fat Ants

Jessica is twenty-four, and it's been six years since I've seen her. It's a dark afternoon in late August, and her house looks empty, just like the rest of the neighborhood.. She told me on the phone that she doesn't have a car, that a neighbor takes her shopping. She sounded terrible.

I knock, and wait, then knock again. Finally, shuffling, and a muffled, "Who is it?"

"It's your father," I say. More shuffling, and the door opens. She looks at me and tries to smile.

"Hi Daddy." I notice the smell before I start to hug her, but I hug her as best I can anyway. I can tell right away that she's too thin.

Inside, the smell is worse, sickeningly sweet with a foul undercurrent. She leads me to the living room, and I sit down across from her. Except for the couch and a chair, the room is empty. Everything seems to be covered in a thin layer of grimy, reddish paste.

"How are you, sweetheart?" I say. I can tell that she's not at all well just by looking at her. I could tell on the phone. She's thin and pale, and her clothes are filthy. I think she's on drugs.

She speaks quietly, "I'm fine, Dad. Just different."

I smile as well as I can and hand her the bag of cookies, the kind she liked when she was a little girl.

"Remember these?" I say. She takes them and puts the bag down on the floor.

"Thank you."

I look around the bare room. "Nice place," I say with a smile, and that at least gets a little chuckle out of her.

"I don't care, Dad. It's not important to me anymore."

"Your mother tells me you've taken up gardening since uh, Steve left."

As she shakes her head "no," I think I catch a glimpse of something black in her oily brown hair, but maybe it's my imagination.

"Well that's what I thought she told me anyway. So what have you been up to?"

Jessica catches up with the conversation at this point, and remembers that her mother and I are divorced.

"You talked to mom?"

"Yeah. Not my favorite thing to do, but I had to get your number from somewhere." She looks tired. Whatever she's on, I just hope she'll be with it enough to understand the things I have to tell her.

"Mom's a bitch," she says, "and you're an asshole."

"I admire your candor, honey," I say, "but I think even your mother and I deserve a little better than that."

"Steve was an asshole, too. That's why I went for him, 'cause he reminded me of you."

"Honey, I really need you to focus. I'm here because I have to tell you something."

Jessica's lips draw back from her teeth and I can see little white flecks of sputum in the corners of her mouth. "He locked me up, you know, in the basement! You remember-"

"Jesus Christ!" I yell, but it's not because of anything she's said - there's a giant black ant crawling down her arm. I point, but she doesn't even look at it.

She continues, more calmly: "You remember locking me in the basement. How scared I was."

"Jess, there's a goddamn bug on your arm. Get it off, now, please."

She finally glances down at the ant, on her forearm now, then looks right back up at me. "I'm not scared anymore," she says.

I stand and lunge for her arm. My fingertips catch her hand, tugging it a little. The ant falls to the ground. I hear something else, almost as small, hit the floor at the same time. Jessica looks to whatever it was, and shrieks.

I move quickly to finish the thing. It's on the floor, two steps away. It's one of those fat ants, the kind with sections so full that they glisten like pieces of perfectly-ripe gray-black fruit. My foot goes down on top of it, and it's over. No contest.

I look back to Jessica, and she's standing up. She's sobbing. She's picking whatever fell back up off of the floor. I step closer to her. "I'm sorry, honey. I didn't mean to scare you."

She doesn't hear me, or she pretends she doesn't. She tosses the object onto the chair. She reaches behind her other elbow. Something is wrong with her arm.

"I'm sick," I tell her. There, it's out. If I have to tell her a few more times before she understands, that's fine, but I have to settle it now. "The doctors say-"

"I don't care, Dad. It's not important to me anymore."

"What do you..." I stop. Jess has removed the clip from her other arm and her flesh sags down, much looser than it ought to be.

"They told me it would hurt, but it didn't. They know where the nerves are. They can tell everything."

She reaches back to the base of her neck. For a moment, I think I know what has happened. I think that she must have lost an incredible amount of weight, that her skin is loose because she used to be bigger. But then the clip at the neck goes, and there's no more explanation. Her features fall away into a pool of skin. Her scalp falls to one side, so that all of her hair is on the same side of her head. She pulls apart the skin that covers her mouth.

"When you kill one, they know. And that's when it happens. They told me all about Steve. You think they don't know, but they know a lot of things."

I can't speak. I can't move. I've never seen a human being that looks like my daughter does now, trapped in an enormous bag of skin. But over the course of a minute or so, her looks start to even out again. I think it's an allergic reaction. She looks like a balloon that's being pumped up. Then, as her hair re-centers on her head, I start to see the tiny movements below the surface of her skin. Swimming, rippling.

As my mind reels toward the enormity of the truth, I look for something and find it at the exact same moment. A bandage hangs from a dime-sized hole in her ankle, and thousands and thousands of ants are swarming into it.

Jessica fills up quickly. She coughs, and dozens of ants fall out of her mouth. One clings to her lip, and goes right back in.

I can hear myself talking, but I have no idea what the words are. She can't speak, but I can see her trying to smile. She's bigger than I am now, and stretched almost to the breaking point.

I can't remember losing my balance, but I'm on the floor. My little girl grabs me by the scruff of my neck and picks me up off the ground. My muscles refuse to do my bidding and I can only surrender. Five steps to the open door, then I'm rolling down the stairs to the basement. The door closes, and it's dark.

My leg hurts when I try to move it. I can hear the terrible tiny sounds, but I can't see anything at all.

After what seems like many hours, the door at the top of the stairs opens again. Jessica turns the light on. Her skin is all back the way it was, and she looks like she's ready for bed.

"You want something to eat down there, Dad? How about some cookies?" She throws the unopened bag down the stairs. "I'm not a part of your life anymore, Daddy. I told you, I'm different now."

"Jess, please-"

"You never left the light on for me, but I'll leave it on for you. Anyway, I want you to see what's going to happen."

"Can't you please, just, we can work this out-"

"Uh-uh. Goodnight, Daddy." Jessica closes the door again.

The ant mound in the basement is at least eight feet high, an ant Tower of Babel. I'm able to put the story together in my head, at least enough to understand my fate. That's got to be Steve over there - picked clean. Now, as the sentries have reported back and the army marches towards me, all I can think about is what a terrible father I've been. Good God, I've been a terrible father.

Pizza Castle

"Okay, guys, what do you want for dinner tonight?" said Mrs. Lime.

"Pizza,"said Mikey.

"Pizza sounds good," said Mr. Lime.

"PIZZA!" yelled Jordan.

"Alright, that was easy. From where?" said Mrs. Lime. Mrs. Lime liked pizza, too.

"Checkerboooard," said Mikey. Mikey was twelve, and fond of the status quo.

"How 'bout Pando's?" said Mr. Lime. Mr. Lime was a connoisseur of pizza - the thicker and more unusual the better.

"No way! I want the CASTLE!" said Jordan, "Remember, Mom, you promised? The castle!" Jordan was four, and he really didn't care about pizza at all. He wanted to go to the castle.

The castle was Lenny's Castle of Pizza, a local eatery with somewhat interesting decor and terrible pizza. Mrs. Lime and the others tried to remind Jordan that they'd actually had take-out pizza from Lenny's before, and Jordan himself hadn't enjoyed it much, but to little effect. Jordan whined and banged his head on the floor until, one by one, his family members shrugged and decided that maybe the pizza at Lenny's would be better this time.

Lenny's Castle of Pizza was a larger place than it looked from the outside. The kitchen ran the length of one whole wall, and then the other wall was the castle. In between were a dozen or so tables, and, along the back wall, some video games. But the castle was the main attraction. It was very realistic looking - even close up, it was hard to tell whether it was really made of stone. There was a painted moat which children could cross over a wooden drawbridge, and inside were at least a dozen kid-sized rooms (including a below-ground dungeon decorated with plastic skeletons), a ball pit, and two turrets with windows and sliding boards leading back down to the tables.

As the Lime family made their way inside, Jordan made a beeline for the castle. "AAAAAHHH! CASTLE!" he screamed. While Mikey got a table, Mr. & Mrs. Lime went to place their order.

Lenny Walton was forty-four, a tall, skinny man. He liked pizza as much as anyone, but his passion was the castle. Lenny and his employees wore costumes made of real chain-mail, and all but Lenny complained about how heavy and hot they were. Lenny completed the look with an oversized ring on his left hand, with a black stone that stuck out half an inch or more.

"My, what an unusual ring," Mrs. Lime said.

"Thanks," said Lenny, "I like it, too. Plus, it's magic."

"Okay, so I'm looking for the list of toppings..." said Mr. Lime, "What's the selection like?"

"Cheese, pepperoni, sausage, mushroom, onion," said Lenny, "You want any other ones, you gotta bring your own."

"No peppers, even?" said Mrs. Lime.

"Not even green peppers?" said Mr. Lime.

"Pepperoni," said Lenny, "Any other ones, you gotta bring your own."

Behind them, Jordan screamed with delight again.

The windows in the turret were small enough to keep just about any average-sized kid inside. But Jordan, being both smaller and more agile than average, had somehow managed to slip through. He hung by one hand, ten feet up, shrieking at the top of his lungs. Mr. and Mrs. Lime ran toward their son. More than a couple of other parents took an interest as well, and knocked each other out of the way trying to reach him in time. In the end, however, no one did make it in time, and Jordan fell to the floor head-first.

"By the thunder of Malagon," said Lenny, "That's not good."

The other parents cleared the way as Mr. and Mrs. Lime approached Jordan's limp form. He was breathing, but his eyes were closed. Mr. Lime kneeled down over his son, and Lenny came out from behind the counter.

"Call an ambulance," Mr. Lime said to Lenny, "He's out cold."

"Please," said Mrs. Lime, "Oh God, I think he's really hurt."

"No way," said Lenny, "I'm not gonna do that."

"What are you talking about?" said Mr. Lime.

"He fell, you hunk of crud," said Mikey, kicking at Lenny, "Call an ambulance, you butt."

But Lenny just stood there, shaking his head "They'll wanna take my castle, and I like it too much."

Mrs. Lime took out her phone and dialed 911. Mr. Lime stood up towards Lenny, a severe look on his face. "Paul, don't do anything stupid," said Mrs. Lime, "Jordan's already hurt."

Mr. Lime clenched his fists. "You..."

"I'm sorry I can't help you. I think you better leave."

Mrs. Lime spoke to the emergency dispatcher "Our four-year-old son is hurt, he's unconscious."

"Wait, who is she calling?" said Lenny. "You guys better just leave."

Mrs. Lime stood up from Jordan, tears streaming down her face. "We're at Lenny's Castle of Pizza," she said.

As if the words were magic, Jordan opened his eyes.

"Our lawyer will be very interested..." Mr. Lime said.

Coming to, and realizing where he was, Jordan jumped up like his pants were on fire. Everyone in the restaurant stood by in awe as he took off across the drawbridge again.

"CASTLE!"

Lenny's feeling of relief was obvious. He smiled at the Lime family. "Don't worry, I'll get him," he said. Lenny stooped down and entered the main gate of the castle.

Mr. Lime looked at Mrs. Lime. "Is that a good idea?" he asked. But before Mrs. Lime had a chance to answer, a metal gate slammed down, and the wooden drawbridge started to pull shut. Forty seconds later, the castle was secured, with Jordan and Lenny on the inside, and everyone else on the outside.

While Lenny hadn't wanted something like this to happen, he had been well-prepared for it. He knew the castle well, and simply pushed the other kids along through the rooms, then into the turrets, and down the slides, which were then closed off with iron bars. Lenny wanted to send Jordan down the slide, too, but Jordan pulled away and ran back into the castle proper. He really wanted to stay.

The employees of Lenny's Castle of Pizza were anything but loyal, and were happy to call the police on their employer. The police arrived promptly, and the restaurant was evacuated. Only the Lime family stayed.

Inside the castle, Lenny opened a secret passageway that gave him access to an underground wing of rooms that Jordan hadn't seen before. In one was a TV with a video game system. In another was a cache of real medieval weapons as well as a bunch of modern military surplus stuff. Jordan made himself at home.

A regionally famous hostage negotiator, Orville Black, was called in to make contact with the alleged kidnapper. Over the wall, Lenny explained to Orville that all he wanted was to be left alone in his castle. Jordan was free to go anytime he felt like it. In fact, Lenny wished that Jordan would go so that he would finally have a chance to play Renegade Battle Crunch 3. Jordan was bogarting all the cool stuff, and had already made short work of his stash of snack cakes.

The SWAT team tried a standard battering ram, but had no luck infiltrating the castle. No one knew how it had gotten there, but the small castle was in fact made of stone. The doors were thick and sturdy, and the windows were few.

At four a.m., Orville Black gave up and went home, his reputation tarnished forever. He came back a few hours later, and tried to get back on the case, but by then the time for negotiation was over.

The Limes cried and pleaded, but the best they could get out of Jordan was a snort: "I don't need to come home. I'm at the castle. It's good food, and fun."

Mr. Lime tried to remind Jordan of the story of Pinocchio, and how he'd been turned into a mule for not taking care of his family responsibilities and just having fun all the time, but Jordan had never watched that movie, and was too involved in a high-scoring game of Renegade Battle Crunch 3 to be bothered.

On the second day, the police decided to send in tear gas to get Lenny and Jordan out. The Limes protested at first, but finally agreed it was a small price to pay to get their son back. Of course, Lenny and Jordan had been anticipating this move, and had their gas masks on before the first canister landed. After that plan failed, the chief of police decided there was no other option: they would have to call in the Marines.

The first thing the Marines did was to open the top of the strip mall like a tin can. Then they knocked down the walls that surrounded the castle. When it stood alone like this, exposed to the elements, the castle looked much bigger than any of Lenny's regular customers might have imagined.

The Marines attempted to lay siege to the castle. One team pounded at the front gate, while another tried to get in through the roof. Lenny tried to ignore the Marines and concentrate on the TV, but Jordan was adamant about defending his new home. When Jordan threw a potato that caught a Marine officer in the forehead, an invisible line was crossed. The officer got in touch with the Pentagon, and the mission was changed. While the military had originally shown up to liberate Jordan from the castle, their only intention now was to reduce the castle to rubble.

Mr. and Mrs. Lime tried to protest, and even got their lawyer on the phone, but there was nothing they could do - that single act of potato-throwing defiance had upset someone high enough up the military ladder that an emergency tribunal had been called where Jordan (and Lenny, by association) were instantaneously and unanimously labeled "enemy combatants" and an imminent danger to national security.

A man in a uniform spoke into a bullhorn, and laid out Lenny and Jordan's options. It would take approximately twenty minutes for the Air Force bomber to arrive, and during that time, either or both of them could surrender themselves into military custody and waste away in an offshore prison indefinitely. Or, once the plane had reached its destination, (assuming they survived the initial blast), they could take their chances with the ground troops, who were under orders to take no prisoners.

Inside his private bunker, Lenny thought about his choices. It wasn't supposed to have gone this way. Whether the kid was in there or not, they had no right to bomb his castle. Jordan came in and turned the television on. Lenny turned it off again.

"Listen," said Lenny, "I liked this castle, but you made it stupid, and now they're gonna wreck it."

"We can take them," Jordan said. "Lock and load." Neither of them knew what "lock and load" meant, but Lenny knew that expecting his castle to withstand bombing by the Air Force was asking too much. He would have to take the most evasive action possible.

Lenny took the big black ring from his finger, and threw it to the ground. The jewel broke open with a champagne-cork-like pop, and a cloud of blue smoke rose from the floor. A tiny, ugly man with a long beard appeared. "Hey, whutsup?" he said.

"I want to get out of this castle deal," said Lenny.

"You know you'll have to give up on castles," said the short, ugly man with the long beard.

"Forever?" said Lenny.

"And ever," said the man.

"Me too?" said Jordan.

"Kid, you can do whatever you want. But if you're here when we switch it around, you'll be affected, too. No way around that. So listen, Lenny, maybe you'll like something else later in life, like hamsters or garages, but you've exhausted your castle privileges. I'm not doing any more castles."

"But I like castles," said Lenny.

"You could always try your chances with the bald guys," the little man said.

"Lock and load!" Jordan yelled.

"Ah, forget it. Let's get out of here," said Lenny.

"Okay, no backing out," said the man. And that was it.

So just as the Air Force bomber was about to drop its first bomb on Lenny's Castle of Pizza, the castle disappeared. The plane disappeared. Lenny and Jordan and the rest of the Limes and Orville Black and chief of police and the Marines all disappeared, and everything went back to the latest common denominator, that is, to the latest possible moment before any of this had happened. Except this time it was different.

"Alright. That was easy. From where?" said Mrs. Lime. Mrs. Lime liked pizza, too.

"Checkerboooard," said Mikey.

"What about Pando's?" said Mr. Lime.

"No way! I want the IGLOO!" said Jordan, "Remember, Mom, you promised, the igloo?!"

Jordan whined and banged his head on the floor, but this time, none of his family members would budge on the issue.

After all, everyone knew that Lenny's Igloo of Pizza was a joke as far as the pizza was concerned. They didn't even have ovens.

The King of Antarctica

August 8th, 7:30 PM

I hate this stupid town. Every time a mom & pop goes under, another ugly chain store, donut shop, fast food craphole takes its place, until it looks like every other stupid town in America, and soon every other stupid town in the whole stupid, ugly world will look just like this one. It's disgusting.

Anyway, my computer's back up, and I got a new phone, but I'm ignoring them both for a few minutes here to work out my issues on real live paper, like my ancestors did. The two weeks my computer's been down have actually been a really productive time for me. I've been getting plenty of sleep, been on time to work every day. I've been doing my hair…

So here's the thing: two weeks disconnected has taught me that I don't ever want to go back to where I was, attached to a computer every second of every day. For like years now, I've been sitting at a computer at work all day, then coming home and just getting on the computer and pretty much never ever doing anything else. There's almost never anything worthwhile on any of the sites I look at. It's all just sucking my soul until I die.

So instead of messing with any of that stuff anymore, I'm gonna write my book. I've been meaning to write one since, I don't know, high school at least, right? Yeah, at least. So tonight's the night I get started. And my goal is to have a first draft in six weeks. The research I've done tells me it shouldn't take any longer than that if I'm working on it every day, and really, what excuse have I got not to? Not a real world social life, that's for sure.

I mean, I could have a real world social life if I wanted one, probably. The past couple of weeks reminded me of what that's like a little bit.

Phil at work is interested in me. He halfway asked me out today, told me about some show he was going to, and asked me if I wanted to meet him there. I didn't say yes, but I halfway

would have, if he hadn't done it in such a half-assed w.
Anyway, I'm gonna be busy with this book and stuff as soon as
finish this little missive and boot up the laptop.

Sorry, Phil, you suck..

It's a good thing I won't be on social media tonight, 'cuz I'd
be at least tempted to talk about him and what a loser he is,
couldn't even ask me out like a normal person. And I know I've
gotten in trouble doing that before, so good thing I won't be on.
Anyway, I do kinda like Phil, he's not a creep or evil or anything.
But in the real-time real-world right now right now, I need to
keep it all about me.

So then I saw on my phone (in the ten seconds I had to
check it at lunch time), there's this new free game out today,
"The King of Antarctica." It looks like a sim-despot thing where
you try to take over countries and it's got these underwhelming
retro graphics. I know it sounds like it's right up my alley, but
I'm gonna be strong.

My book is gonna be about… Well, what genre should it be?
A western? An old west populated only by kickass girls? Nah,
that's too good an idea not to have been done to death.

I want to say before I even start that I'm only playing this
game for like half an hour, and only for tonight. I've got a LOT
of book to write, and I didn't even really get started yet here.
Also, I've got a tendency to get a little involved in games like this
and that's the last thing I need right now. Did I say a little? Yeah,
a lot.

And I need to get up and feed the cat.

August 21, 11:15 PM
The computer crashed, and the phone is still charging. Just
read my last entry - guess I didn't get started on that book just
yet. Phil finally ended up asking me out more officially, and
declared his intentions or whatever, but I said no. That guy's
borderline psychopath full of himself, man, he's no fun at all.
Anyway, I've been really busy, with the book coming up and
Jesus, more than anything, more than everything, dear god, the
King of Antarctica! Gotta tell you. I've been playing pretty much

a week or two. Morning, lunchtime, all night, and
ds so far. I can't believe I'm not done with it yet.
lay is so simple, but so fun - you conquer pretty
city on earth, one at a time. I've just made it up to
King of all of Paraguay, and it's getting late but I've got a lot
more shit to conquer before I sleep, more shit to conquer before
I sleep.

Come oooon - why's it taking so long? I'm also finding out a
lot of new strategies as I go along. Different ways to arm and
organize the hordes. The sucky part is I can't find any forums
that have tips or anything. It's just a bunch of people asking each
other how the game is, and nobody playing it and then coming
back to say how awesome it is. I guess that makes sense, since
the game's so addictive... Holy crap, I just thought up the plot
to my book - the heroine goes around murdering people that say
"addicting" instead of "addictive." Instant worstseller. Anyway,
I'm learning as I go. I can't really imagine that many other
people are playing it. Nobody could've gotten as far as I am
now. No serious gamer kids would put as much effort as I have
into a game like this. Mark my words, I will be the first female
King of Antarctica, and very soon.

October 7, 5 AM

I almost forgot about this notebook. CPU crashed. I'm the
King of Brazil, the King of Mexico, the King of the USA,
Russia, and China. Unfortunately, there's no way to tell how
much farther I've got to go. I checked out a map of the world
online at work, but I couldn't tell really how many cities are left.
But it couldn't be long now, could it? Also, for the last week or
two, I've been having these dreams about Antarctica just about
every night. About being there and freezing my figurative nuts
off. There's a castle and I'm visiting the king, right? But every
time I dream about it, the king is a different person. He's always
a different little hacker kid, and the old kings, the other different
hacker kids, they're not dead or anything, they're all in the
throne room crowd.

When I checked that map, I also found out a little bit about Antarctica. There aren't any cities, supposedly, and only a few dozen people live there.

So when I get to that point in the game, I'm not expecting there to be any cities there. I mean, when I click the mouse to engage Antarctica, it's gonna be just the one item there, and it's the whole continent. That's when I'll know I'm about to win.

Damn, I keep meaning to post somewhere about the cat running away.

October 14, 6:13 PM

I got pulled over coming home from work.. "Inattentive driving," the douche said, and I didn't even wreck, didn't even hurt anybody. I swear all these cops want to do is keep people from using their phones while they drive, even when we do it responsibly. I was going below the speed limit, even, but no, "inattentive driving, Miss." You don't know me, you forty-year-old loser, maybe I'm married and I just don't wanna wear my ring... Asshole! I can't wait to... what, even? I don't know how it can ever get better. Ugh, I just hate this place- no one's on my side, ever!

BUT!

There's no 'i' in team, but you know where there is one? Antarctica!. My computer is my friend, and that's all I need. Purrrr.

October 15, 10:25 AM

I was supposed to be at work today, but I'm really closing in. My dreams are all screwed up now: there are a couple hundred people down there, including some women now. So I'm not going to be the first girl king, huh? Half-second bummer when I figured that out, but screw it, I've come this far. The castle's all made of ice and everyone's huddled up together there, but they've got parkas and stuff. I think it'll be comfortable enough...

Tonight there was another new king, and he was probably only like 14 or something. Like King Tut, you know?. So every night it's a new king, and now everyone down there keeps talking about future conquest. Future conquest... weird, right? Since the new King of Antarctica always just took over the rest of the world? What else is there?

October 16, 6:02 AM

I finally made it. I'm here. One click to start the engagement, then maybe three minutes before I'm off on my journey south, to be the King of Antarctica until someone else wins.

I've been briefed. They told me last night what's going on. There's nobody I don't like down there. That's my people, and we're taking over. Nothing will ever be allowed to get on my nerves again when I'm KING. Nobody's been posting on the forums cuz nobody knows shit about what we're really up to. People on forums are assholes, and the game is not only not for them, it's not a game at all.

I know the people down there are like me, because I'm gonna tell them the same thing all the other kings have been telling them. I'm gonna tell them how our top priority has to be taking over this town. How the people here are like people everywhere - they don't care and they've got to go. Of course, when I say "taking over" this town, I mean we're gonna lay the fucker to waste - we're gonna wipe this piece of shit place off the face of the earth. Then let 'em call me "Miss"!

Maybe when it's all over, someone will find this book in the rubble and get an idea that I was the one who ripped this place a new one. Then again, once I've exacted my full vengeance, there might not be any rubble left..

The Swimming Pool

Outside the supermarket, Alvin saw a couple of kids on bikes. They couldn't have been more than eleven or twelve, but the expressions on their faces made them look like old men. *They must have some pretty heavy stuff going on to look like that*, thought Alvin. They reminded him of his own childhood, and the whole thing with Joe and Teddy. He let the memory surface in his mind now, but in a safe way, as a single chunk of experience wrapped in enough plastic that the feelings couldn't seep through. These kids on the bikes could almost be Joe and Teddy, Alvin thought, if their bikes were different, and if they were dressed the way kids had dressed when he was young.

Alvin's mind pulled back several layers of wrapping on the memory. It dragged him back to that day, the day he'd lost his comb, that day at the swimming pool. The supermarket hadn't been there then. Not even the shopping center in those days. Just the train tracks and trees and a wide open field all the way to the old neighborhood. And the swimming pool.

The swimming pool was just a hole really, less than ten feet deep, a twenty foot square edged with railroad ties. Presumably, the railroad folks had dug it to put something in (or maybe they'd taken something out, who knew?) and just left it there. The kids thought it was full because of the rain, but none of them really knew. The water was cold, and smelled like the railroad, oily and bad. Whether it was tar or charcoal, or just dirt, there was no way you could so much as dip your big toe into the swimming pool without it coming out covered in grit.

As Alvin loaded his groceries into the car, he heard one of the kids by the edge of the building yell: "That's 'cause you're a puss!" The other kid responded, but it was too low for Alvin to hear. He watched as they continued back and forth, and it made him smile. The smaller kid was rationalizing, trying to get out of something the other one wanted him to do. *Talking about it won't work, pal,* Alvin thought, *you either do it or you're a puss.*

The kids looked around to see if anyone was watching. Alvin pretended to go about his business, but he didn't take his eyes off of them. They headed back behind the building.

Alvin's mom had hated the whole idea, and had forbidden him to go. He'd made it in a few times anyway, but the water always gave him away: not only would a dip in the swimming pool cover your skin in that gritty film, it would permanently stain your underwear gray, like you'd washed it with new black socks. Alvin had gotten in trouble every time he'd gone in.

He knew where the kids were going. What else was behind the supermarket? He shoved the rest of the groceries into the trunk and drove back to the loading dock. There was no sign of them, just the employee parking lot and a fence. It shouldn't be

48

far from that fence to the pool. Maybe a hundred, hundred and fifty yards...

No, that was crazy. It would be long gone. Why would a thing like that still be there? Especially after what had happened.

Alvin parked the car. He clenched his teeth. He was just going to have to go back there and find out.

Joe and Teddy were brothers. Alvin had been friends with both of them since his family had moved in. Their mom worked, and their dad was gone, and they would be at the swimming pool every day of the summer, to say nothing of spring and fall, and sliding across it in the winter.

But that summer had been different. Teddy had ratted Joe out over some dirty magazines they'd found in the woods, and both of them were grounded for the whole month of July. Their mom would call at various intervals during the day, and if no one answered, there'd be hell to pay when she got home. They were smart kids, though (at least smarter than their mom gave them credit for being), and before long, Joe and Teddy figured out the pattern to her calls. They felt confident leaving the house for short periods to play outside, but they never dared venture all the way to the swimming pool. By the middle of the month, though, Joe and Teddy's mom had relaxed on the calls a bit, and she hadn't called on a Monday yet, so the boys decided to chance it. That was the day Alvin lost his comb.

The sun had just gone down, but Alvin could see well enough. On his way back, he could just follow the lights for the supermarket. He tried to be quiet; he didn't want to scare the kids, he only wanted to see if the swimming pool was still there. The kids themselves didn't matter - he'd mostly forgotten about them. He figured the matter of the smaller kid's respective puss-ness (or not) probably involved a routine introduction to substance abuse.

Alvin found the trail through the woods right away. He hadn't been near this place in twenty-some years, but even in the fading light, he found his way easily.

Alvin knew that combs weren't expensive. But this had been an official barbershop comb in a brown plastic pouch that his dad had bought him at the actual barbershop. Alvin discarded the pouch right away, but he carried the comb in his back pocket everywhere he went. It didn't matter that he didn't use it, it was the principle of the thing. He was proud of that comb, and it was his.

Joe was already swimming, and they were both trying to get Alvin to go in. Teddy probably still had a lot of work to do to get back on Joe's good side after that thing with the girly mags. Otherwise, he never would have taken it.

Alvin felt less comforted than he thought he would to see the place again. From the trees, he could make out the shapes of the kids sitting on the railroad ties that made up the edge of the swimming pool. Except for their voices, everything was quiet.

"It's creepy here," said the first kid.

"No shit, Sherlock," said the other.

"I like it sorta though."

"You know a kid died here one time. No, wait, yeah, it was two of them."

"Yeah, you're full of crap, too."

"Uncle Steve told me. One kid drowned and the other one just got killed by a murderer or something."

Alvin stepped out into the open. "That was a long time ago," he said.

He heard both kids exhale. They stood up, but they didn't run away.

"I'm sorry, did I scare you guys?"

"No, we're good."

"Mister, we're not doing anything, we were just…"

"Lighten up, you guys, I'm not a cop," said Alvin. He walked over to the edge of the swimming pool, about ten feet from the two boys. "You know, when I was a kid, we used to go swimming in there."

"How deep is it?" one of the kids asked, but it was getting too dark now to tell which one.

Alvin looked down into the pool, and couldn't see anything but black. Same old swimming pool, he thought. He wondered if his comb was still down there. "I don't know. It's not all that deep. Probably eight feet, something like that."

"Do you really know that story about the kids?"

"Yeah, I know it..."

"Will you tell us?"

Alvin sighed. "Okay." He kicked a rock into the pool, and the splash brought the whole thing back.

"They were brothers. One of them got hurt and fell in the water. The other one died trying to save him."

"What happened to the first kid?"

"He got hurt. And then he fell in the water."

"What kind of hurt did he get - exactly?"

Alvin squinted at the kids in the dark. There was no reason not to tell them the truth. "He threw my comb in the water, and I threw him in."

"Screw THIS!" said the smaller kid. And then he was gone, scampering away into the blackness. Halfway to the trees, he yelled to his friend: "Come on!" But the other kid stood his ground.

Alvin smiled as he continued. "I was as scared as they were, you know. When he hit his head on the way in, I saw my life flash before my eyes. Then his brother tried to save him, and they tried to get up, but..." Alvin shook his head.

"Then what happened?"

"I just really didn't want to get in trouble for going in there. I didn't want to go in there. My mom would've gone crazy."

The kid kneeled down by the water. Neither of them said anything. Alvin heard a car drive by in the distance. Once it passed, everything was quiet again. Then tiny splashes. The kid was dipping his hand into the water.

"What are you doing in there? Aren't you scared like your friend?"

The splashing stopped. "You mean my brother? You're joking, right?"

"No..."

"Then ha ha don't make me laugh, we're not scared of you. The question we all wanna know is, are you scared?"

"Yeah I'm scared," said Alvin. "I've always been scared."

The kid stood up and walked closer to Alvin. He held out his hand in the dark. "Here, I found this. I think it's yours."

"Yeah, thanks. I was wondering what happened to it."

Alvin heard the rush of small feet behind him, and turned around just in time for the push.

The water was just like he remembered it being. Cold, and dirty.

Peanut Butter Elvis

"This is so boring. Don't you have any other flavors?"

I hated it when she said things like that, especially to people she didn't know. The guy behind the counter didn't seem to mind, though. He probably got ten or twelve customers like her a day.

"Well, if you can't decide, just go with an old standby. When's the last time you had vanilla? Or french vanilla?"

We never think about the regular flavors, and I was about to ask the guy the difference between vanilla and french vanilla, but Bernadette wasn't having any of it.

"Boring," she said, then rapped so loudly on the glass case that I thought sure it would break. "Whaddaya got that's *different*?"

Personally, I go for Rocky Road every time. There's lots of tasty stuff in it, and just as important, I never wind up in situations like this, where I'm unable to decide. But Bernadette is Bernadette. She's got to have her ice cream, and it's got to be weird.

"Cherry Butter Brickle?" the clerk tried.

"Didn't like it."

"Almond Apple Crunch."

"Are you kidding? That stuff tastes like an old tire." We'd been in this situation before, more than once, and every time, Bernadette had finally been able to decide on a flavor. Sometimes I finished my ice cream first, but she'd always been able to decide eventually.

The clerk threw his arms up in the air. "Here's a concept-maybe you just don't like ice cream."

Bernadette glared at the kid. She wasn't going to hit him, at least I didn't think she was, but she couldn't let him get away with a crack like that, either. She lowered her voice. "I love ice cream. I think the problem is that this store is just... lousy. You don't care about ice cream, ice cream cones, ice cream eaters, ice cream... scoops. You don't... Come on, Albert, we're leaving." She grabbed me by the ear, the way she does when she's mad at the world. It hurt, but I tried not to complain. Underneath it all, she really was a good person. She pulled me towards the door.

"Wait!" said the clerk, "I have an idea." Bernadette turned around.

"What?"

The clerk smacked the side of his own head like it was a malfunctioning dishwasher. "I don't know why I didn't think of it before."

"Okay, okay, what is it?"

"A new flavor, an experimental formula. The boss left me just a couple of scoops in the back- I was going to try it later."

"We don't want to take your-"

"Shut up, Albert. What's it called?"

"Peanut Butter Elvis."

Bernadette's face lit up in a way it usually only does when she's unwrapping a gift, or dreaming about unwrapping one. "What's in it?"

"It's ice cream. Highly experimental, but ice cream."

"Gimme both scoops, as much as you got."

The clerk tried to insist that it was too early in the testing process for Peanut Butter Elvis to be eaten two scoops at a time, but being insistent against insistence is Bernadette's specialty. So she did get her way, but not before we both signed a specially-prepared waiver disclaiming responsibility for "death, dismemberment, memory loss, hair loss, or any or all other ailments great or small" experienced after trying Peanut Butter Elvis. I wasn't sure I wanted to sign, but I didn't want to cause a scene.

Once the document was signed (and notarized - evidently you needed all sorts of special qualifications to work in this ice cream shop), the clerk went into the back of the store, and emerged moments later with a large waffle cone containing almost two scoops of normal-looking ice cream.

"This is it?"

The clerk nodded. Bernadette took a lick of the ice cream, and nodded to me. I ordered my Rocky Road, and paid, and we left.

In the car, Bernadette said something I'd never heard her say before: "Elvis Aaron Presley was born on January 8th, 1935 in East Tupelo, Mississippi."

"Is that right?" I said, "I'd wondered about that sometimes. That's the same Elvis Presley that was a rock singer, right?"

"Elvis began his professional singing career at Sun Records in Memphis in 1954."

"You don't say," I said. But she did. She kept reciting more and more facts about Elvis. After she went through the basics, she started right in on the ephemera: Elvis's weight at birth and death, intimate details of his love life, and the number of Cadillacs he gave away to fans. That night before we went to bed, instead of giving me a list of things I had to do before she woke up the next day, Bernadette told me that Elvis Presley had been nominated for 14 Grammy Awards, but had only won three. And then she fell asleep.

She woke up in the middle of the night, got a glass of water, and said "In 1957, Elvis performed five concerts in three Canadian cities, but that was the only time he ever performed outside of the United States." I didn't know that, and it seemed odd to me, since she'd already mentioned the names of all the different countries where Elvis had hit records.

In the morning, though, Bernadette was herself again. She sent me out to the bank, to the grocery store, and to get some ice cream. To my surprise, she actually wanted the Peanut Butter Elvis a second time. It wasn't brand new anymore, but if it was okay with her, it sounded great to me. I skipped my other errands and went straight to the ice cream store. After all, if I could get Peanut Butter Elvis again, hopefully more of it this time, my other errands would presumably take care of themselves.

The same clerk was working, and he smiled when he saw me.

"Peanut Butter Elvis, right?"

"That stuff is a miracle. In one day it's completely turned my marriage around. I'll take as much as you've got."

"I'm sorry, we don't have any more."

"No! Call your boss, please! I need it!"

"I'm afraid he's decided to cancel the Peanut Butter Elvis project."

"What? No! I need it! I'll pay any price."

"There's too much potential for abuse with a product like that. Of course he wants to make money, but he says he won't take responsibility to turning the world into a bunch of Elvis-fact-spouters. He says we'd all be crazy in a week."

"Not me, and anyway, I don't care about the world –it's my wife I'm worried about. I'll sign a waiver- anything! Please!"

"Okay, calm down. All is not lost. We cancelled Peanut Butter Elvis, but we've decided to go forward with a similar flavor. It's just as potent, but less likely to cause a worldwide catastrophe. And just because I like you (and because I met your wife), I'm authorized to give you a special deal if you buy ten gallons."

"Absolutely, ring it up."

When I got home, Bernadette was extremely upset with me.

"Albert, you fool. I told you to buy some pretzels and some mozzarella sticks, not just ten gallons of ice cream."

"I'm sorry, dear. I don't know what I was thinking."

"You should be sorry. You should be hung by your neck until you die!"

I scooped out a big bowl of the new flavor. "Correct as always, darling. Of *course* I should be put to death. Now just relax and have some ice cream and before long you'll feel better about the whole thing."

Bernadette sniffed at the ice cream. "This isn't Peanut Butter Elvis." She took a bite. "It's pretty good, though. What's it called?"

Suddenly, Bernadette sat upright in her chair. She looked at me. Her face contorted just a bit.

"Vincent Damon Furnier was born in Detroit, Michigan, on February 4th, 1948," she said.

I let out a big sigh, and kissed Bernadette on the forehead. Then I danced a jig and kissed her again, this time on the mouth. It was going to be a good year. I had ten whole gallons of Chocolate Chip Alice Cooper.

Glaxxon

"Hey boy, don't pee on that." Paul Overmeyer tugged on Leon's leash. He pulled the dog off balance, but effectively kept him from lifting his leg on the wooden picture frame leaning against the garbage can. What was that thing anyway? He walked Leon the rest of the way down the block, and kept thinking about it.

Paul never dug through trash piles himself, but he knew how it worked: when someone has something good that they want to get rid of, a passable hunk of furniture or a working TV, they leave it out by the trash a day or two early. Someone almost always comes to claim it before the trash man does. Paul himself had gotten rid of several things that way (including his ex-wife's mini-trampoline), but before today, he had never seen anything of much interest in anyone else's trash. No matter what the picture looked like, that frame seemed pretty good.

On his way back, Paul took a good look at the neighbor's house. The curtains were closed, of course. Even though he'd lived on the street for several years, Paul had only seen the man who lived there a few times, and then only when he was leaving. The neighbor was a tall, redheaded guy with a beard. Paul had never even said hello to him, but now he was about to pilfer something from the man's trash.

Paul felt a little nervous about turning over the picture, but there was nothing on it. The image area, about one by two feet, was covered with a brown grocery bag, taped down on all four sides. Paul glanced again at the neighbor's house before picking up the picture.

"We'll have to open it when we get home, Leon boy."

The unveiling was anticlimactic. It was a very boring landscape: a picture of a well near a barn with some woods in the background. It was nicely done, and painted in oil even, but there wasn't much to it.

"Yup, a well," Paul said. And now that he was examining it, the frame wasn't as great as he'd thought it was either. It looked like some gravy or something had been dripped on it at some point; there were brown stains all across the bottom of the frame.

The painting was signed, though, so at least that was something: in clear red letters on the bottom edge, it read: "Glaxxon '86."

Glaxxon. That was an unusual name. Paul headed for the computer. Since he'd been living alone, he'd kept his computer on the kitchen table, so he could surf the net while he ate. It made more sense than eating in another room.

Glaxxon (War Glaxxon, actually) wasn't a listed artist, but he was still active, and he had a website. The paintings on Glaxxon's website were sort of dark in subject matter (castles, chains, and naked people, mostly) and expensive, too, or at least Paul thought so. The street address for Glaxxon's studio was in Indiana, pretty far from where Paul lived in Connecticut, but there was an email address. After reading Glaxxon's cryptic, presumably self-written biography ("...Glaxxon's art is life itself." "Glaxxon knows your truth…" "Glaxxon can never die."), Paul deduced that the painting of the well he'd plucked from his neighbor's trash was a very early work by the artist. If Paul had been disappointed by the picture of the well, he was even more disappointed with the rest of Glaxxon's work. "I bet he'd want this back," Paul said to himself, and set out to type an email.

> Dear Mr. Glaxxon,
> I happened to find an early painting of yours (a well near a barn from 1986) in my neighbor's trash. I don't usually go through trash, but this picture seemed worthwhile and so I brought it home. I don't dislike it, but it doesn't match the other things in my home, so if you would like it back, I'd be more than happy to send it to you.
> Sincerely,
> Paul Overmeyer

The reply came less than an hour later:

> Mr. Overmeyer,
> Yes, thank you.
> Glaxxon

Glaxxon's email also included the same address listed on the website for the studio in Indiana. The reply seemed abrupt to Paul, but he took it in stride. Maybe Glaxxon wasn't such a good guy (and from his website it seemed like he wasn't), but maybe all he needed was a little kindness to turn him around. Maybe when Paul sent him the picture, it would help him get back in touch with his younger self - the self who preferred painting wells and barns to painting naked people chained up in castles. Maybe it would be a turning point for Glaxxon, and he'd go back to painting nicer things. To Paul, it felt good to be nice to someone, whether they really appreciated it or not.

That night, Paul had a dream about the well in the picture. In his dream, Paul approached the well and looked down into it. Inside were naked people in chains and broken mirrors and evil goats. His ex-wife was also in the well, and so was Leon, and the naked people in chains and evil goats were not at all nice to either of them. Paul woke up sweating. He was glad the picture would be gone the next day.

The next day was Wednesday. Paul wrapped the picture carefully, and took it over to the post office during his lunch break. Paul thought the clerk at the post office might ask embarrassing questions, but she barely glanced at Paul. He sent the package second-day, so that Glaxxon would have it on Friday. Paul wondered whether Glaxxon would bother to send another email to acknowledge his effort, or if he would have to rely on the tracking number.

Saturday afternoon, as Paul walked Leon, he was surprised to see his tall, red-bearded neighbor. The man was lying out on a blanket, sunning himself in the yard. The red-bearded man called out to Paul, and they took up a friendly conversation. His name was Alex, and he looked as though he'd never been out in the sun before. Alex wondered about the weather, and Paul told him what he'd heard. Alex asked about Leon, and Paul told him that Leon had been his wife's dog, but that Paul had gotten full custody in the divorce.

"Change is tough," Alex said, "but not always bad. If you'd told me on Monday that I'd be where I am now, I'd have spat in your eye. And today, I'm a changed man. Happy and free."

"How so?" Paul asked, but Alex fell quiet.

"Um... I..."

"I'm being nosy. I apologize," Paul said.

"No, it's fine, it's just not something I can talk about right now - it's too close."

They left it there, but the two men shook hands and wondered why they'd never talked before. Both said what a fine thing it was to have good neighbors and all of that.

Around eight o'clock that night, just as the TV was getting good, Leon barked, and Paul heard someone knocking at his door. He wasn't expecting anyone. He pulled his robe on over his pajamas.

"Who is it?" Paul said.

"A friend, bearing gifts," came the reply.

Paul was light on friends, particularly the sorts of friends prone to showing up with gifts unexpectedly, so he figured it must be Alex from down the street. He opened the door.

Paul didn't recognize the man standing before him in the yellow porch light. He was short, with long scraggly hair, but Paul noticed right away that he was dressed very sharply, with an electric-blue bow tie.

"May I help you?"

"Are you Paul?"

"I am."

"I'm from Glaxxon. I've got some things for you."

"You're kidding."

"Nope. I'm really from Glaxxon and I've really brought some things for you."

"What do you mean, things?"

"Just some money, and some other things. Can I come in?"

Paul had always admired men who wore bow ties, and aspired to someday build up the nerve to wear one himself, at least once. He opened the door. He had to pick Leon up to keep him from barking too much. "Sure. Happy to have you."

They went into the kitchen. In the light, it occurred to Paul that the man seemed short because he wasn't fully grown yet. This certainly wasn't Glaxxon, or anyone else born before 1986. He seated the young man at the table and went to the refrigerator for some lemonade.

"So what's your name?"

"I'm Gartharoid of Glaxxon."

"Gartharoid? That's an unusual name."

"I come from an unusual family."

"And you're his son?" Paul said.

The young man looked at Paul.

"War is my brother. I've brought some stuff for you. Three gifts for one well. That work okay for you?"

Paul handed Gartharoid the lemonade and sat down. "You know, I really was happy just to return the painting," he said, "As you can see, it really wouldn't have worked in here."

"You're not the well type."

"No, I guess not," said Paul.

"No. You're not." The young man moved over to the other seat, in front of Paul's computer. "May I?"

"What do you mean?"

"Looks like a cool computer, can I check it out?"

"For..."

Gartharoid shrugged, "Do you have any good games?"

"Does solitaire count?" Paul asked, chuckling at his own joke.

The young man smiled gently and put his finger on the computer's power button. "Is it okay?"

"Sure," Paul said, and the young man turned the computer on.

While the computer was booting up, Gartharoid stood to unbutton his suit jacket. He produced a thick kraft paper envelope. He opened it and dumped the contents onto the table in front of Paul. There was a wrapped stack of paper money, a cd in a paper envelope, a folding knife, and a small golden crucifix. Gartharoid picked up the money first, and held it out to Paul. "Here's a thousand dollars."

Paul hesitated. "My goodness. Why are you giving me a thousand dollars?"

"Glaxxon likes the well," he said, "You know, maybe you should count it."

"What do you mean?"

"I mean, you don't know me, what if Glaxxon sent you a thousand dollars, but Gartharoid swiped eighty off the top."

"Why would you do that?"

"Maybe I'm a dumb kid and I don't know what I'm doing," said the young man.

Before Paul had a chance to reply, the computer made its startup noise. "Yes!" said Gartharoid, "Time for Blanksies."

"What's Blanksies?"

63

"It's a great game. You play it with a gun and you point it at someone and spin the barrel and see if you get Realsies or Blanksies, get it?"

Paul looked concerned. "I don't think guns..." he started, but Gartharoid interrupted him.

"It's a computer game. So addictive." He picked up the cd from the table, "I have it here with me, do you want to play?"

"I don't know, about guns..." Paul started again.

"It's not a real gun. Nobody gets hurt. It's a video game. Can I just play it for a minute? It's fuckin' fun, man."

"I don't like that kind of language," Paul said

"Okay, okay, look. You count the money, I'll play one quick round, and then we'll go out and have a drink." Gartharoid pushed the button to open the disk drive and put in his cd.

Paul smiled at this. "I don't think you're old enough to drink," he said.

"Ah, you got me there," said Gartharoid. "Ten more long months before I turn twenty-one. I just thought, you know, if the money's all there, maybe since you've got a lot of money and I've got nothing at all, maybe you'd buy me some beer. Because maybe I got sent here with nothing but what I'm supposed to give you. And maybe I've got a great game that I really like, but no computer at home to play it on, and that's the size of it. So, if it's okay, count your fifty twenties slowly, let me play one round of Blanksies, and I'll get out of your hair. I promise not to bother you any more than that."

This speech made Paul think. "You know what, Gartharoid? I'm sorry," Paul said, "I didn't think of it being like that. So take ten, fifteen minutes, play two rounds of Blanksies. Whatever you want."

"Thanks, Paul, that means a lot," said Gartharoid. Then he looked back down at the screen. "Holy shit," he said, "what is this?"

Paul leaned over to look at his computer. The monitor showed only wavy lines going sideways.

"Is it your game?"

"No, it's your computer. I know the cd works, it works on my dad's computer fine. I don't even know what to do."

"I don't know, either," said Paul, "Try turning it off, then turning it back on again."

"Ugh, I'm not gonna get to play my game. Ah, man, Paul. Your computer sucks." Gartharoid removed his cd from the tray. He tried to smile and pretend it was okay, but Paul could see that he was upset.

Paul went back to the refrigerator and took out two beers. He usually only drank one a week by himself, on Friday night, but having company made this a special occasion. He really didn't approve of serving alcohol to a minor, but the kid had mentioned beer before, and Paul hoped it might put him in a better mood.

This plan worked, and soon Paul and Gartharoid were across the table from each other again. The computer was trying to reboot, but having trouble. The young man picked up the crucifix and handed it to Paul. "This is from my dad."

"I thought you said he was your brother," Paul said, smiling.

Gartharoid took a swig of his beer. "I say a lot of things, Paul. Sometimes I don't even know myself what's true. Anyway, it's been in the family for a while. I think it's valuable, but I don't know for sure. Are you religious?"

"Not terribly," said Paul, "But I can appreciate something like this. I wouldn't think your father is very religious either, after all those pictures I saw…"

"Don't let those pictures online fool you. War Glaxxon's a very religious man. And he pays his debts - that's why he wanted me to give you this."

"It's lovely. And unlike that painting, I feel like this piece really will find a home around here."

"Good," said Gartharoid, "and I hope you'll feel the same way about my knife, though I doubt you will."

The handle of the pocket knife was made of orange plastic. It looked like some sort of military design. Paul picked it up. "This is your contribution?"

"My dad made me pick something that meant something to me. I got it from a buddy of mine who went overseas and never came back."

"I'm sorry."

"I'm not. He was a jerk. Hard to feel bad for someone who's not suffering anymore. I've always liked this knife, though."

"I think about those complicated sorts of situations a lot," said Paul, "when my wife and I broke up, I thought it was the end of the world, but you just keep going anyway. And sometimes it... really hurts."

"Yeah," said Gartharoid. Then he stood up. "Well, I gotta get going. Can I have another beer for the road?"

Paul gave Gartharoid his last beer, but worried about him driving. Strangely, though, when the young man left, Paul didn't hear a car door slam or an engine starting up.

Paul thought a lot about Gartharoid. About how tough it was to be a young person today. So many pressures, so many worries. When he heard the sirens half an hour later, he hoped that his young friend was okay. Paul thought briefly about where he would hang the golden crucifix, but he left it on the table with the knife and the money.

The police came the next morning and took Paul away. The arresting officer's dog had just died, and so Leon was able to avoid the pound. The evidence stacked up against Paul neatly.

There was a missionary who had been to Alex's house on Friday, and he identified the golden crucifix. The two of them had purchased it together at a local antique mall on Wednesday. Another neighbor had seen Paul and Alex talking together on Saturday afternoon. Alex had taken exactly a thousand dollars in cash out of the bank on Saturday morning, fifty twenty dollar bills. And then there was the murder weapon, the orange-handled pocket knife, which had been wiped clean, but still had enough of Alex's blood on it to identify.

In court, Paul's lawyers tried their best to talk about Gartharoid and Glaxxon, but it didn't go well. Even though Paul's computer wasn't working, they were able to retrieve the pair of emails from the cloud. That might have helped Paul's case, except that War Glaxxon lived in Indiana, and was childless. Also, an unsigned, undated painting of a well near a barn was found in Paul's back yard, in the frame he'd described, and the jury had a hard time believing that this wasn't the painting he'd plucked from the trash, if that had ever really happened at all. They also noted how little the painting looked like a Glaxxon.

In prison, Paul heard stories about other people who'd crossed paths with Glaxxon. He'd never had a chance.

Nothing Concrete

It wasn't cool at all. I'm not sure how I let this woman drag me up there, or why, but there she was, maybe four hours after I'd first laid eyes on her, jumping around on the ledge on top of the Potter Building.

"Tomas, look at me! I am a magical dancer!"

My name is Thomas, and I prefer Tom, but what she called me sounded more like "toe maaahs." I really hated it, especially since she should have been calling me Mr. Baxter.

"Get down from there, you idiot," I said. "You're gonna fall and break your stupid neck."

"Tomas, look, I can fly. Want to see?" No. I didn't want to see that. Not even a little bit. It was 11:30 A.M. and I was still a little hung over from all the gin rickeys I'd had the night before. I'd lost any number of secretaries for any number of reasons, but this one took the cake. I covered my eyes.

"Wheee..." I heard the voice trail away. I opened my eyes and she was gone.

There's no way to prepare yourself for a moment like that. Usually when you meet someone who's off their nut, they'll at least put up a sane front for a day or so, but this girl hadn't even done that. It had been, "Do you know how to go to... roof?" "Let's eat on the roof," and after I'd grudgingly accepted, "Wheee..." and I needed another new secretary. I'd really have to talk to personnel about this. They'd sent me some winners before, but this time, holy moley, what could they have been thinking?

I spent a few minutes getting my story straight. I mean, god forbid, someone might think I pushed her, or that I was trying to get at her and it went wrong. The situation seemed poised to blow up in my face. I didn't look over the edge. I'd seen enough crap like that in the war to last me forever, no way I'd look at it on purpose now.

When I got down to the office on the 73rd floor, she was already there waiting for me. She smiled, and I could have wrung her neck.

"You little sneak. How'd you get past me?"

"I flied. I went to Rio de Janeiro and went to the market there." She noticed that I wasn't smiling, but I'm not sure she understood it was because of her. "I brought you a flower."

She handed it to me. I'm not a botanist, but it was pretty, I guess. She was a liar and a sneak, but there are worse crimes in the world, and giving me a present isn't one of them. I looked her over right where she stood, and thought about it. Maybe I could overlook glaring insanity just this once. Her filing seemed okay, and she was very nice to look at.

At the end of the day, she told me she'd be coming home with me. Since I hadn't drawn the line at deceit and jumping off of buildings, I saw no real reason that any line had to be drawn at all. Once we were comfy and cozy in my exotic love den, I tried to press the issue about what had happened on the rooftop, but it didn't seem to get through. She just kept kissing me and saying my name wrong - "Tomas, Tomas..."

She left before sunrise and met me at work right on time. At lunch, once again, she wanted to go up to the roof. I tried to talk her out of it, but she didn't pay much attention. I couldn't blame her for that: as pathetic as it sounds, by lunchtime on day two, I was already just along for the ride.

Sure enough, as soon as we'd finished eating, it was time for her magical dancer jazz again.

"Come on, Tomas. You can fly too."

"No. I'm sorry. I really can't."

"We'll go to Rio de Janeiro. It's a beautiful city of love and romancing."

"Yeah, I've been there. It's pretty cool."

"Well, I am going to fly." So stupid, I thought. You can't do that. But that's all I had time to think before she jumped. "Wheee..."

This time, there could be no doubt. She had actually gone over the side of the building. I had to look over the edge. Maybe there was a balcony ten feet down or something else soft she might have landed on. Nope. Nothing. Just the empty-looking street far below. I felt dizzy.

I got myself together, figured out my alibis again and took the elevator down to 73. She wasn't there. Next I went down and looked for a crowd on the street around where I thought the body should have been. I looked up. Where had we been? Right there? It was hopeless. In a blind panic, I ran around all of the adjoining blocks, just in case she had somehow fallen over another building. There was no sign of her, or anyone who'd fallen off of a building anywhere. I headed back to the office. This time, she was there waiting for me. She looked serious.

"Tomas, I must talk to you."

"Yeah, okay, in my office."

"No," She said. She pointed up, and I knew what she meant.

When we got to the roof, there was a young man waiting there. She explained, well, from what I could understand, as they were both speaking quickly and not always in my language, that his name was Jose and the two of them had met on a street corner in Rio and instantly fallen in love just moments before.

"Jose is not afraid to fly," she said.

"We are magical dancers" said Jose as they both pranced up onto the ledge.

"Well, I'm sure you'll have a good time together," I said.

"Jose is not afraid to fly. We are not afraid, Tomas."

"I can see that."

From the way they looked at each other, I could tell we wouldn't be repeating the previous night's feast of Eros anytime soon. I watched closely this time, and when they jumped, they didn't fall straight down, but away from the building. And when they'd reached a certain speed, they started going up again, then over the top of the building next door, and away out of sight.

I looked out over the edge of the Potter Building. Was that all it took? Just to get up there and dance around, then jump off and fly? And even I could do it? Nah. Not today. Not me. I turned my back to the ledge and headed down to give the personnel department a piece of my mind.

The Breathing Lady

They drove to the back of the cemetery. Patty pulled her rental car off the dirt track between some trees near the edge of the river. It was early afternoon, and no one else was around.

Lunch had gone fine for Patty, and on the ride over from the restaurant, she had finally steered the conversation around to what she really wanted to talk about. Susan told her right away that she was glad it was "safe in the ground with mom."

Susan was only nineteen. She'd brought her dog with her, a teacup poodle named Mitzi. Patty talked Susan into leaving Mitzi in the car - they parked in the shade, and left the windows down. Mitzi barked twice as they exited the car, but their departure was otherwise silent. Patty followed Susan across the graveyard.

"So," Patty said finally, "She was buried with it?"

"Sort of," said Susan, "Not exactly."

Susan had never met most of her mother's family. She remembered meeting her grandmother once, when she was very young. But as she'd told Patty on the phone, she didn't remember meeting her Aunt Joan at all.

Patty didn't look like Susan's Aunt Joan, but her coloring was similar enough, and if Susan had any suspicions, she hadn't let on. They'd hugged, and they'd swapped stories that only relatives would tell. It helped that Patty knew plenty about the Woods family, and it made sense that she would. They had all lived on the same block forty years ago. Joan and Margaret (Susan's mother) lived on the corner with their mother, and Patty's folks lived a few houses down. Patty had been friendly with the whole family. That's how she'd found out about the Breathing Lady.

Patty had only seen the Breathing Lady once. Margaret and Joan knew where it was hidden and had taken it out of its glass jar in their mother's wardrobe. The eyes had tiny corks stuck in them, and the girls knew they weren't supposed to remove them - it was bad enough that they looked at it at all. They'd told Patty everything they knew about it: it was a family secret, passed

down from mother to eldest daughter, and it could bring back the dead.

When Patty saw Margaret's obituary in the annual class letter, the story came back to her. She thought of her own mother, already in hospice, and knew what she had to do.

"Here we are," Susan said, stopping in front of her mother's headstone.

Patty closed her eyes and bowed her head. After a while, she looked up again. Below the dates, the stone read "Beloved Mother." Patty pressed her lips together "It's really nice," she said.

"They did a good job, didn't they?" Susan said. It occurred to Patty that this was how it went - people in a graveyard will do anything to avoid talking about the dead. Patty didn't say anything, just nodded through her grimace.

"Thank you for being here, Joan," Susan said, "I'm glad you're here."

"I know it's weird..." Patty started, "But I just wonder..."

"The Breathing Lady again?" Susan's voice was guarded, but that didn't mean she wouldn't tell Patty where it was. Anyway, Patty was growing weary of being so nice to the girl. Susan had bought Patty as Aunt Joan, and that gave Patty the clout she needed. Now they would have a friendly family conversation about it.

"It's important to me that I see it again."

"Well, you know you're not supposed to-"

"I know it goes to the oldest. But you're the oldest, too. So that means it's yours, right?"

"I guess, in a way," Susan sighed and sat down in the grass.

It was a beautiful day, and Patty noted how pristine Susan looked; except for her squinting into the sunlight, she looked like a model in a lawn care ad.

"You know Mom said it was okay to bury it with her," Susan said.

"But you said it wasn't, exactly."

"Right, it wasn't exactly. But that doesn't mean I want to go digging it up. What do you want with it, Joan?"

"It belonged to your grandmother. It was always important to her, important to your mother, important to me: it's an heirloom. And it just doesn't seem like it's very important to you."

"I don't feel good about this," said Susan, "having this conversation here."

Patty had one more card to play, one final emotional plea, and just about enough steam to do it. If it didn't work, she'd come back at night and figure out where it was. But it would be much easier if Susan showed her.

So Patty thought of her own real mother, how the stroke had left her, and how she only had a day or two left, if she hadn't died already. She slumped down next to Susan, and the tears came easily.

"When I think about my mother... You know I left home early, but... things were different then. I was going to have a baby, and my mother never spoke to me again..."

Patty felt Susan's hands on her own, and knew immediately that she'd won. She silently thanked the real Joan for providing such a convenient story, and the generation gap for being so predictable.

Patty continued: "I just thought, somehow, if I had the Lady, even though we never did in real life, in a way I'd feel like we'd made peace."

"I'm so sorry," said Susan, "I didn't know. I guess Mom just never told me that part of the story." They hugged again. Then Patty looked longingly again at Margaret's headstone. She wasn't being subtle, but she didn't much care.

"It's here," said Susan, "It's right in front of the gravestone, maybe six inches down. But I didn't bring anything to... dig with..."

"I've got some gardening tools in my trunk," Patty said, "Thank you, Susan. So much. You have no idea what this means to me."

Patty went to the car, and Susan sighed again, stretching back on the grass. Susan hadn't told Aunt Joan how scary this was for her, what a relief it had been when The Breathing Lady was finally buried. She hadn't told her about the argument she'd had with her dying mother, how she'd begged her to let it be buried with her, to let the whole business to be over forever. It seemed no matter what she did, her responsibilities kept creeping up on her.

When Patty returned with the spade, Susan asked, about Mitzi, "She doing okay in there?"

"She's fine, you didn't hear her bark or anything, did you?"

"Do you think I should get her some water? I probably should."

Patty stood in front of the gravestone, gardening gloves on, ready to dig. "Can you show me the exact spot?"

"Yeah, hang on a minute, I'm just gonna get Mitzi some water."

"Fine," said Patty. She yanked up a large section of the sod and started to dig. Now that she had a real idea where it was, she had no intention of hanging on another minute.

At the car, Susan pulled Mitzi out through the window, and poured some water from a bottle into her hand. The dog lapped up just a bit of it. As she passed Mitzi back into the car, she noticed Aunt Joan's purse on the floor. Her wallet was right on top. All morning, she'd had a vague suspicion that something wasn't right, but couldn't think of any reason this woman would want to impersonate her Aunt Joan, unless it was because of... That thing she'd been trying so hard to ignore.

Susan looked back across the cemetery, and saw Joan pull up a shovelful of dirt from her mother's grave. She picked up the wallet. This would be her only chance to find out for sure.

Righteous indignation wasn't really Susan's style, but she felt she had to summon some as she approached Patty again. "I'm gonna call the cops," she said.

Patty reached down into the hole and touched something metal. "What's it in?"

"A... mayonnaise jar," said Susan, "But don't you touch it. I'm gonna call the cops."

"What for? I'm not going to break it," said Patty.

"Criminal impersonation. That's a crime!"

"Maybe it is, maybe it isn't."

"And anyway, theft. You're trying to steal something that's not yours."

"Am I really? I think I'm just digging a hole to put some flowers in in a big public place."

"This isn't a public place, it's... I'm calling the cops."

"Don't do it, Susan. They'll think you're an idiot. You're not going to miss the Lady. Just wait until I'm gone and call for a ride home."

"Well... what do you want it for? At least you can tell me that. Look, will you just stop digging for a second and talk?"

Patty reached down into the hole again, and this time, she pulled out the mayonnaise jar, intact. She held it up, but the object inside was wrapped in paper towels.

"You came all the way from wherever, and made up this whole thing. You did it for some reason. Are you some kind of occult freak, or what?"

Patty started to unscrew the lid, and at that, Susan took a tentative step closer. "Don't open it, okay? Not here. If you're gonna take it, go ahead. I'm not gonna stop you. Believe me, I don't want it. I don't know if any of the stories are true, just please don't open it here."

Patty turned her back to Susan and removed the lid from the jar. She put her hand inside and pulled out the mass of paper towels. She dropped the jar on the grass.

"I'm gonna go get my dog," Susan announced. She started walking towards the car.

Patty unwrapped the object until it lay on a single sheet in her hand.

The Breathing Lady of Denmark was only about three inches high, a likeness of a woman's head and shoulders in solid pink. It seemed to be made of stone, but it was hollow, so maybe it was just heavy glass. There were hints of flowers in her wavy hair. Her face held a tiny smile, and her eyes, which had held tiny corks the only other time Patty had seen her, were empty pits, the only openings into the figure's hollow center.

Patty stared at the tiny figure. The eyes were strange - had it been a container for something at one time? Did it work by the air that circulated inside? No matter, as long as it worked. This was Patty's salvation, the solution to her main life issue. When her mother was gone, the Breathing Lady would bring her back to life. Probably not forever, who knew for how long, but she would have some more time. Patty held the statue to her ear, half-expecting it to literally breathe, but she heard nothing.

Patty re-wrapped the Breathing Lady, then located the jar and the lid and sealed her back inside.

Susan came back with Mitzi.

"Did you look at her eyes?" Susan asked. "You know you're not supposed to do that."

"I never saw her eyes before," said Patty, "But it's okay." She looked towards the car. "Anyway, I've got to get going."

Patty took exactly three steps toward the car, then dropped the jar with the Breathing Lady inside. She turned right sharply, and marched toward the river. Susan watched her go.

"Aunt Joan would have known not to look at her eyes," Susan said.

By the time Susan reached the precipice and looked down, all she could see was the river. There was no sign of Patricia Grace, whoever she had been.

Susan carried Mitzi and the jar with the Breathing Lady, and walked home that day. It was only a couple of miles, and she didn't mind the exercise.

The next week, Susan got a call from the cemetery, telling her that her mother's grave had been "tampered with." They didn't give any details, but Susan's best guess would have been right on the money. Someone had been walking by and seen the hole where the mayonnaise jar had been buried and when they looked down into it, they saw Susan's mother's dead hand, exposed, but still below the surface level.

Susan asked the question, and was told that no other graves had been disturbed. She was glad to hear that the Breathing Lady hadn't done more damage.

Once she got off the phone, Susan sighed. The Breathing Lady would be hers now, until she could pass it on to a daughter of her own. It would be better that way.

The Way to Gregory's

If you don't have anywhere to go, they pretty much just drop you off. It's tough to sleep the night before you get out, so I fall out pretty hard in the car. The dude yells in my ear to wake me up, then without saying goodbye, he lets me out on a street corner I don't recognize. I don't care about saying goodbye to him, either, since he gave me the info I needed at the start of the trip. So I'm figuring I'm in New Haven, somewhere. I've got to figure out where I am, and then I can get over to Gregory's. I've got eight dollars in my pocket, same as when they picked me up thirty-eight months ago.

I don't have a watch, and the battery on my phone is long gone. Even if it wasn't, my plan is. I'm guessing it's around seven in the morning. Nothing going on yet, no traffic or anything. I walk down the street, but it's hard to even get my bearings about what part of town I'm in. There isn't much trash on the sidewalk, so I've probably got a long ways to go to get to Gregory's. I'm guessing with that, because I've never been to Gregory's place before. I should probably catch a bus over there. Looking for a stop now. I can talk to the driver and figure out where I am.

I'm hungry as hell, too. I didn't miss this part of the outside, where you're responsible for what you're gonna to do next. In jail, you know you'll get your squares. Still, not like it's a toss-up, I'm smilin' to be out in the open air.

I've walked at least five blocks now, and I haven't seen anyone, not even somebody collecting cans. There's parked cars, but I haven't seen a moving one yet. I keep walking downhill until I see a big open park. How about that? Beautiful. I could spend the day there, just relaxing. Probably beg enough change to get a hot dog and keep my eight bucks. I can sleep in a doorway somewhere and catch the bus tomorrow. Sure, Gregory's could wait. Not like I've had a whole lot of adventure fun recently.

I'm looking forward to seeing some real-life girls, too. I don't even want to talk to them, just look at 'em and smile. I shaved last night, but I haven't showered in a week, so I probably don't look too bad, but I know I smell. So at this point, my plan for the day is pretty much set: I'm gonna smile at some girls and lie in the grass.

When I get to the grass, it's still wet, so I won't be lying down in it until later. I walk over to the drainage ditch and look down over the guardrail. There's a long slope, maybe 30 feet or so before it levels off, with four or five inches of clear water running down it. It must have rained yesterday. If I'm gonna be outdoors overnight, I'll have to get used to rain again.

It seems weird that nobody's around yet. The sun is warm, and I find a bench. A newspaper would be good now, right? I look back the way I came. No little stores or restaurants, nothing. Just the park and a whole lot of residential as far as I can see. I lay down on the bench and close my eyes.

I dream about the guards in the prison, what bastards they were. "Lets go rattle some cages!" I actually heard a guy yell that from far off one night, before they busted in and knocked a bunch of us around.

When I open my eyes, the sun is sticking out over the tallest building nearby. I sit up. It's gotta be ten o'clock by now. I look around across the field, and into the streets. No cars, no people. I'm still the only one around. Where the hell is everybody?

"Hello?!" I yell out to the people who ought to be there. They don't say shit, and how could they? Whatever, that works for me, 'cause right now I'm going to go take a bath. I measure the jump into the drainage ditch, and it doesn't look too bad. I take off my shoes and roll up my pants. I see a spot to stash my clothes right across the way, and an easy place to climb up on the other side. If I fall and crack my head, it might be a long time before someone finds me, but nothing good will come of thinking about that.

I land on my feet at first, but the water's running pretty strong, and it knocks me down.

"Shit" is the first of twenty or thirty words I rattle off. I get back up on my feet okay, but me and my clothes are both soaked. I'm more used to cold water than I used to be, but that doesn't make it pleasant. I'll have to wring my stuff out and put it in the sun.

I'm just starting to strip down when I hear a lady's voice behind me:

"Hey! Do you have any food?"

She's halfway inside one of those giant drainpipes. She looks scared. She's about my age, and I can tell she used to be cute, but her right eye is puffy, red and yellow; some kind of infection in it. I don't have any food, and I tell her so, but I guess it's a strange enough situation for both of us that we keep talking anyway. She doesn't want to tell me much of anything or come out of the pipe, but when she invites me, I put my shoes on and follow her inside. I have to stoop just a little to walk in the pipe, and I'm glad she's got a flashlight. We go along for a while before I think of the right thing to say.

"Look, is this New Haven, or not?"

"New Haven?" she laughed, "No. It used to be South Haven, but now it's not called anything. Nothing is." Seems like a weird thing to say, but then she explains how she thinks everyone but her and her friends is gone. She doesn't give me a chance to guess why.

"Trolls," she says. "At least I think they're trolls. They look pretty normal except they're about 15 feet tall." I ask her what she's been smoking, and she tells me that they don't smoke anything in the sewer where they live, 'cause they're scared it will attract the trolls. I ask for more details, of course, and she actually has, or makes up, more. Ten or fifteen of these trolls showed up in town two winters ago, and started wrecking everything, flipping over cars, body-slamming people on the concrete, biting their hands off, stuff like that. The government was in on it, or wanted to cover it up, because they faked footage of a train carrying powdered cyanide blowing up and killing everyone in town. Now all the roads in and out are closed, and good old South Haven, Connecticut is a mostly-barren troll-state. The idea that this could happen with no one on the outside finding out seems sketchy and impossible, but what the hell do I know?

The lady talks for a good long time about this troll stuff, and all the while we're going deeper and deeper into the tunnel. The craziness of the situation isn't lost on me, that a few hours ago I was in jail and now I'm walking through a sewer listening to someone I don't know talk about how trolls have taken over the world. Finally, she shines her light on a big grate door that goes across the whole tunnel. There's a padlock on it, but she's got the key.

"You're welcome to come in, you'll just have to check in with Walter," she says, "Also, supplies are very low, so I hope you weren't expecting much to eat."

I don't really know what I was expecting to find down there, but those bars clinch the fact that I haven't found it.

"I'm not going in there," I tell her.

She thinks I'm stupid not to. "It's the only safe place," she says.

"I can't be that kind of safe anymore."

She steps inside and closes the grate behind her. "Suit yourself. Just don't come running down here when the trolls try to eat your goddamn face."

"I promise not to," I say. "Hey, can I borrow a flashlight for the way back?"

"I can't," she says. I don't wait for her to say anything else. I take off in the direction we came. The tunnels suck without a flashlight. I keep falling down. It seems to take hours to reach the entrance again, and maybe it does- when I finally come out, the sun's right overhead.

I work my way up the other side of the ditch like I'd originally planned. I didn't get to take my bath, but maybe now there will be some people around and I can finally figure out where to catch a bus. I'm not at all afraid of trolls, but the situation with that girl with the bad eye has me creeped out enough that I want to at least get away from where she was.

As soon as I clear the barricade on the opposite side of the drainage ditch, I see the overturned car. It's a shock after what that lady just told me. I know I can drop back into the ditch right now or I can keep going forward into the unknown. I decide to go forward.

There aren't any people in the car, but I do find a sealed package of crackers. Pretty good, too. Those people in the sewer aren't trying very hard.

I turn a corner two blocks on, and hear techno music. I follow it, keeping an eye behind me for an escape route. Just as I reach the top of a hill, I see, far away, some dude sitting on top of a car with his back towards me. I don't yell out to him yet, but as I get closer, I can see underneath the car, and it looks like his ass is on the roof with his feet touching the ground. That's a tall dude, really tall.

There's a boombox on the ground next to the car, turned up all the way. I realize then that if that lady was telling the truth and there really are trolls around here, they must have a huge bunch of regular people stuff that they can't use- not just because they're so big, but also because there's only ten or fifteen of them taking up this whole area.

I crouch down to watch him, and the first thing he does is sniff the air, then turn around. He looks right at me and smiles.

He stands up all the way, and I lose my breath. His face is really big, but it looks like a person's face mostly, so maybe he's a giant, not a troll, but that point's moot now. He picks up the boombox with one hand and throws it at me like a football. It flies at me in slow motion, and the music gets louder as it comes closer.

The radio hits the ground ten feet away and I'm running at full speed though an alley. It's a poorly-thought-out escape route, from a more innocent time a minute ago when I didn't believe in the thing that's chasing me now. I want to look back and find out how close he is, but that will take time, and I have a speed disadvantage already. As I reach the other side of the alley, I decide to chance it. I glance back, and the alley is empty. So

I've got at least fifteen more seconds to live, that's pretty good. But not necessarily true.

The giant steps out and blocks my path. He's been waiting for me - went around the block the long way. There's over-matched and then there's over-matched, and that's definitely one or the other.

"What are you doing out here, little man?" the giant says. His voice is so deep that it's hard to understand.

"I don't want any trouble. I'm just trying to get to my man's house," I reach into my pocket and pull out the paper with Gregory's address on it.

"No trouble at all," the giant says, snatching the paper out of my hand with two fingers, "Lemmee look at this." As he looks over the yellow scrap, I get a better look at him. The clothes he's wearing look like people clothes, and they fit him normal, but he's got no shoes on. He's seriously about fifteen feet tall, and could squash me, if not flat, at least dead, without much effort.

"Do you know Gregory?" the giant asks.

"No, the cop gave me his address, told me he'd take care of me, give me a job."

The giant hands the paper back to me. He doesn't look like he's about to kill me.

"What was the cop's name?"

"I don't know."

"I have a hard time keeping track, too," he says, "I'm Gregory."

"Christopher," I say. We don't shake hands, but he nods at me a little bit.

"Listen, Christopher," Gregory says, "I've got a people problem."

"In the sewers, right? And you can't fit in there?"

"Yeah."

First day out, and I've got a job and a meal ticket, short-term security, and, most likely, buildings full of apartments I can look through just for fun, legally this time. I smile at my new friend.

"Let's go rattle some cages!"

86

The Girl on the Corner

The girl on the corner has her hands in her pockets. She chews gum as she waits for her boyfriend to arrive. The old man is shaky, with a cane, and she sees him coming from a long way off. He seems harmless enough. He shouldn't give her any trouble.

It's almost dark, and a cool breeze blows dead leaves from one side of the street to the other. The traffic is sparse for now, but soon it will pick up, and then the cars will have their headlamps lit. She hopes that Mitch will show up before then.

She expects the old man to shuffle past, but instead he stops cold just a few feet away.

"Good evening, Miss," The old man says, a smile in his voice. The girl keeps looking down the street. She hopes that if she ignores him, he'll go away.

"Good evening," he says again, a little louder, "Can't you hear me?"

The girl nods in the old man's direction, but keeps her eyes focused one block down. "Yeah," she says in a voice almost too soft to hear, "I can hear you."

"What are you doing out here all by yourself?" says the old man.

"I'm waiting for my boyfriend."

"It'll be dark soon - are you sure he's on his way?"

The girl checks her watch. "He'll be here any minute. He must be running late." She snaps her gum and continues to look down the block. She wants more than anything for the old man to move along, but instead, he moves closer.

Over the course of a full minute, maybe more, the old man slogs across the small patch of grass between the sidewalk and the curb. At the edge of the street, he eases down to one knee, then, aided only by the cane and supreme determination, settles himself down onto the concrete step.

At this, the girl takes a step away, closer to the telephone pole.

"If it's all the same to you," the old man sighs, "I think I'm going to just sit here and rest a while."

"It's a free country," the girl says. She wonders where Mitch could be - she hopes he really will come soon.

A gust of wind blows the leaves around some more. On the next block, a trash can falls over. The old man keeps his eyes fixed on the girl.

"The fellow in the store down the street told me a story, about an old lady who used to stand on this corner."

She wants to tell him to go find this old lady, and to leave her alone, but she bites her tongue. Anyway, it shouldn't be long now.

"She was waiting for someone, too. Someone who went away to war and never came back."

"That's a sad story," says the girl. The old man nods.

"So, what kind of a car does your boyfriend drive?"

The girl looks over at the old man. He looks familiar to her somehow- she must have met him somewhere before. Maybe he's a friend of her parents, or her grandparents. And she knows what kind of car Mitch drives, of course she knows, but right now, with the question in front of her, she just can't seem to recall.

"I don't know... what kind of car he drives," she says.

The old man smiles up at her. There are tears in his eyes. "A lot of things happened in the war, and after the war, too. I couldn't come back then."

It's dark now. As the evening rush hour proceeds, passing drivers catch the old man on the curb in their headlights, but some trick of the light keeps the girl hidden from view.

"I never came back," he says, "but I never forgot about you."

The girl turns her full attention away from the street for the first time she can remember. She stares at the old man. He's different, but she recognizes him at last.

"Mitch?" she says, "I've been waiting a really long time."

Acknowledgements

Many thanks to all my people, but especially these ones:

the author A.M. Metivier, for being a powerful and thoughtful mentor.

Marybeth, who came for the cover and stayed for all the pictures. Her artwork is the peanut butter to my story jelly.

Ken Adams, for doing that Ken Adams thing that only he can do.

my wife & family, for their support and inspiration.

Breck Young, a talented artist whose work doesn't appear here.

Thom & Linda Hawkins, who are not at all the characters in *The Truck*. Thom is also not a character in *Nothing Concrete*.

Barrymore Tebbs, a terrific author, who cured my fear of being an overnight success.

Javier Hernandez, for the cool comics and Ed Wood fellowship.

& Dean 'Mojo' Brown, for the tunez.

About the Author

A Delaware native, *Eric Henderson* is the creator of both the world's only anti-Bob Hope fanzine (*SCAREBOB Magazine*, in the early 1990s), and the early 2000s email-only story-zine, *The Frantic Flicker*. Eric spent eight years in Los Angeles, writing screenplays and working in independent film. Now he's married, has a kid, and lives in Connecticut.

Ashes to Ashes, Oranges to Oranges is his first book.

About the Illustrator

Marybeth Chew is an artist in Philadelphia. She loves art, kitties, and playing groovy bass.

To view high-resolution versions of the illustrations in this book, please visit *flickerlamp.net/ashorangeillos*.